PSYCHE UNBOUND

ZENOBIA NEIL

To Planaria and Diane,
thanks for getting me off the ground

PART ONE

MARRIED TO A MONSTER

CHAPTER 1

THE SACRIFICE

Psyche stood alone on the beach, trembling with fear and cold. She had been left as the priest of Apollo commanded, wearing nothing but a red linen shawl and a golden necklace. As the waves crashed onto the sand, she stared at the ocean and waited for the monster to come for her.

Crossing her arms over her chest, she clutched the shawl in her fists, but the thin fabric offered little protection from the wind or her thoughts. The people in her city by the sea had lined the streets to watch the procession, weeping as she walked by with her father and mother and all of their retainers. The little girls had thrown rose petals for her to tread upon and the women had wailed as if they were going to her funeral. Yet it was their adoration that had brought her here.

The oracle had not said if the monster would devour her or keep her for ill-use. Psyche tried to convince herself that dying did not frighten her. Then, at least, she would descend to Hades as a shade and drink from the River Lethe, her sorrow and suffering done. There was very little in her life she wanted to remember.

Suddenly the sand beneath her shifted. The smell of roses and sea spray surrounded her. Psyche felt the presence of an immortal—an essence of pleasure, expectation, and yearning. Making an effort not to gape, she gazed up at the Goddess of Love and Beauty.

One and a half times the size of a mortal woman, Venus towered above Psyche. The goddess's gown was fashioned from dark blue silk and seaweed. The rippled kelp was interwoven with the shimmering fabric, adorned with pearls and seashells, and threaded with pure gold.

Venus was more dazzling than any mortal woman could hope to be, more gorgeous than a man could dream of. Her skin was pure white, like seafoam sparkling in the sun, her lips red and full. Her fair hair, gathered into a complicated bun, glittered as if made of real gold. When the goddess gazed down on the girl, Psyche felt as if she were the only one in the world—until a flash of burning hatred radiated from Venus's eyes—how the goddess detested her!

Psyche knelt and let go of the red shawl, which was taken by the wind. It flew high in the sky, soaring like a bird. Looking down in supplication, her eyes rested on the goddess's feet. Delicate and fine, the most perfect feet in the world. The nails were clear and even, polished like seashells. The ankles trim and the calves full and strong. She dared not look any higher.

Venus lifted Psyche's chin, raising her face to inspect her. The girl was almost blinded by the goddess's beauty though later she could not recall exactly what she had seen—only that the goddess's eyes were blue and angry like the sea. Yet Venus's hand, strong and firm, holding her jaw, made her skin begin to hum with vibrations of pleasure.

Venus pulled Psyche up off her knees and stared down at her with disdain. Psyche's long, golden hair had come undone in the wind and flew behind her. It was shameful for the Goddess of Love and Beauty to see her so disheveled. Venus gathered

Psyche's hair into her hand and wrapped it around her wrist twice, pulling until Psyche bit her lip.

"Beautiful," Venus said. Her voice, even icy with hatred, was like a song. "They all think you're so beautiful. But you're just a little mouse, waiting for a lion."

The goddess cupped the mortal's plump breast in her hand. Psyche's heart pounded in fear, yet the goddess's touch on her hardened nipple brought a bolt of pleasure.

"You expected to marry a prince, little Psyche. But soon a monster will come for you. It will be his claw on your breast." Venus smiled then, a wicked smile. She ran her hand down the girl's slight belly. Pausing at her pubis, the goddess fingered the honey-colored hair.

"Upon his life, your father swore you are a virgin," the goddess said, opening Psyche with her fingers. The cold wind on her exposed flesh made her shiver as the goddess examined her slowly. Vibrations of pleasure coursed through her with the goddess's touch. Psyche dared not pull away as she felt herself moisten with desire as the goddess explored every crevice. Venus's essence overcame Psyche, and she almost swooned with longing as the goddess laughed and slid a finger inside.

Shuddering, Psyche looked into the brilliance of the goddess's eyes until the finger inside her brought a burrowing pain.

"Yes," Venus said. "You will be a worthy sacrifice. Perhaps the monster will take your virginity before he devours you." Venus laughed, releasing Psyche's hair. The girl fell back to the sand on her knees, bereft by the lack of the goddess's touch and terrified by her words.

Tears came to Psyche's eyes. She had not known pleasure until a moment ago. She had not known what it was to be alive until she was about to die. When she dared to look up, the goddess had vanished.

Now the monster would rise up from the sea, or perhaps he would come from the sky and swoop down on her. Clasped in his talons, he would carry her away to his cave, a cold, dark place strewn with the bones of the girls he had had before. The wind roared in her ears. She wiped away her tears and sensed another presence on the beach. He was here for her.

But when she turned toward the rushing waves, she did not see a monster. Instead a beautiful winged man, dark-haired and golden-eyed, gazed at her with curiosity. He was bare-chested, wearing only a silver breechcloth. His muscular legs were tan from the sun, and he held a golden bow in his right hand. She could see the golden and leaden arrows peeking out of the leather quiver on his back, gold for love and lead for hatred. The silhouette of his dark-brown wings was folded against his back. Fearing she had stared at him too openly, she cast her gaze down in fear and saw that his feet were beautiful like his mother's.

The God of Love approached her quickly, a hunter overtaking his prey, but he did not take aim at her with his bow. Instead he slid it over his shoulder, so the bow-string crossed the leather strap of his quiver. Taking her hands, he pulled her close and spread his wings. She stared in awe at the beauty of the feathers, at the span of his wings. Gathering her to him, he pressed her against his chest and began to lift off the ground.

As the sand fell away from her, she struggled against him. In a panic to feel the earth slip away from her feet, she clung to him for her life. Terror of being airborne gripped her. Fearing he would pitch her into the sea, she held fast to him, clinging with all her might. But as the wild blue waves grew smaller, she realized his touch was gentle. Her fear turned to wonder. She was flying!

The blue sea was getting farther and farther away. Above the gray mist of the beach, the sky was blue and the sun warmed her. The wind did not chill her anymore, but felt good against her skin. The sea below, the sky around her, the god who held her; everything was suddenly magnificent.

She became aware of her heart pounding against the hardened muscles of his chest, her pale breasts flush against his bare skin. His embrace warmed her and she stopped trembling.

But as she looked down and saw only his sandaled feet and legs below her, she realized, to her horror, she had grabbed onto him with her legs like a frightened child. Without realizing, she had pressed the most secret part of herself into him. She could feel the moisture of her sex rubbing against his taut abdomen just above his breechcloth. She should let go, should right herself and beg his forgiveness, but she was still terrified he would drop her.

A smile played around his pink lips. His right arm cradled her mid-back, while his left hand cupped her buttock. He removed his arm from her back for a moment and she clung to him more tightly, the softness of her thighs clinging to his hipbones. He squeezed her buttock, supporting her there and kneading the flesh, pushing her harder against him. His touch caused some of the vibrations of pleasure the goddess had given her. Only she did not think it was because he was a god.

She stared into his golden eyes, lost there—unable to look away, for she felt a sensation unlike any she had ever known. Despite already being airborne, as he gazed at her, she felt even lighter, as if her heart and soul were weightless. As she stared deep into the blackness of his pupils, she felt he was made of air, the only air she wanted to breathe.

Suddenly she was no longer willing to die. She wanted to live only to see those eyes. To see herself reflected back in his gaze.

"Please," she said, before even realizing she was speaking.

He smirked with amused patience as he supported her from below. She pressed against him harder and felt the joy of her flesh against his—her erect nipples against his muscular chest, her arms around his broad back, the leather strap of his quiver and the slight string of his bow the only thing between them. He lifted a finger to his lips, requiring her silence and, as he did so, she realized the ocean was gone and they were over land.

She did not want to let go, to be surrendered to her fate. Yet there was no other way. She knew that. But she would not have agreed to die had she known there was this. He put his arm back around her and locked his eyes with hers. It was pure pleasure for a moment, all the more dear for being fleeting. He started to descend. Looking down, she saw that they were above a mountain, inaccessible except by air. She held tight, full of yearning he would not permit her to speak.

He fluttered to the ground softly, but she felt as if she was still moving even when his feet touched the grass. Clutching him, she buried her face in the valley between his neck and shoulder. He stood still, waiting, no longer holding her tightly.

When she did not move, he lifted her off him as if she weighed nothing. She stepped tentatively upon the soft grass and almost fell, but he grasped her hand and steadied her. The moisture she had left on his abdomen glistened in the sun. She should be mortified, yet she was not. She longed to make him glisten in other places as well.

It was unclear what she was meant to do next. Perhaps go on her knees before him in gratitude and awe, or perhaps he would lead her to the altar. If he held the knife, she would not fight if he looked into her eyes while he did it. They gazed at each other a moment—two separate beings, one immortal, the other waiting to die for the crime of being too beautiful.

But he looked away from her, up into the heavens where he would return. He had only come to deliver her to the monster. Now he would leave her to her fate. She eyed his bow, wondering if he would shoot her first. He could be merciful and shoot her with a gold-tipped arrow, so she would love the monster. If he did, she would have a piece of him inside her. But no, he was the son of the Goddess of Love and Beauty, the one who hated her. He could give her no mercy with his mother's blessing. It was more likely he would shoot her so she would love the monster's servant or a tree or rabbit. The goddess would like that. But if he did that, at least she would forget about him, for she thought even if he pierced her with a gold-tipped arrow, and he was the first one she saw, she would not love him more than she already did.

But he did not reach for his bow, did not pull an arrow from his quiver. Instead his wings began to flutter, causing a gentle wind to engulf them both. She reached for him, and he took her hand and pulled it to his lips, kissing the palm tenderly. Then he let her go and rose off the ground. Tears came and she bit her lip to keep silent. She did not want him to remember her, if he remembered her at all, as a coward.

His open wings glistened in the sun as he ascended into the sky. He watched her staring up at him in silence. Perhaps there was pity on his face, but she could not be sure. Then he faded to a speck, and she fell to the soft earth, weeping.

CHAPTER 2

THE MONSTER'S PALACE

"Princess Psyche." A girl's voice roused her. Psyche put her hands on the grass and rose to her knees. A dark-haired slave, her face plain as milk, held out a midnight blue shawl.

"I am Adora, mistress. Please, come with me."

It was cold and Psyche was grateful for the warm woolen shawl. Adora walked toward a line of trees and Psyche followed. All her life, she had seen animals led to slaughter. This was how she felt now. Her feet were like stone, but she followed the slave through a cluster of olive trees with the same resignation as a goat or sheep.

When they came clear of the trees, Psyche gasped. She had expected a bloodied altar, a desolate cave, a hideous monster ready to devour her. Instead, a glittering palace with marble pillars adorned with gold shone in the sun. Saffron silk curtains fluttered in the breeze and there was a light tinkling of bells.

"What is this place?" Psyche asked.

"It is my master's house. It is to be your home, mistress."

Psyche did not understand the other's words. She had expected to be dead by now.

"Who is your master?"

"I do not know. I've never seen him. Come, mistress, food, drink, a bath, whatever you desire awaits you."

Psyche almost laughed. They had all misinterpreted the oracle.

To appease the will of the goddess, Psyche must be sacrificed to a terrible monster, feared by men and gods alike. Her family and kingdom had thought the monster would kill her. But there were many things to sacrifice. Her life was only one possibility.

Her new home was like a temple. A house fit for a god, and despite herself, her heart shuddered. Could it be? No, it was foolishness, a desperate fantasy to take her away from her true fate.

Adora led her into the palace, through the atrium and into the courtyard. The shallow pool in the center was full. She caught her reflection, though she did not immediately recognize herself draped in a dark blue shawl, her hair wild like a grieving woman. She no longer looked like Princess Psyche for, she realized, that was not who she was anymore.

The dining room was bright and airy. It was filled with warm light and the silk curtains lazily brushed the marble floor. The floor was covered in mosaics. Pieces of gold mixed with lapis lazuli, carnelian, and onyx to create pictures that once deciphered, made her blush and then want to look again.

Her father's palace had been the most impressive building in the city by the sea, but now it seemed like a hovel compared to this. The couches were expertly carved with plush purple cushions just waiting to be lain upon. White marble tables with carved lions' feet were laden with bowls of grapes, figs, and apples. Painted vases full of wine and water waited to be served. The drinking cups on the table were golden, shaped like doves, and the whole place smelled delicious. Bread was baking in an unseen kitchen and the fragrant scent of chicken and garlic wafted through the air.

As she wandered through the rooms, she became aware of a familiar sensation. There was a light tickling at the back of her neck as the hair just at the base of her skull rose in silent acknowledgement of something unseen. She was not afraid, nor had she ever been any of the times she had felt this, only curious that it had followed her here. The air around her was slightly charged with electricity, the way the air was before a storm. She had long thought she imagined this sensation of not being alone, of someone unseen watching her.

The first time this had occurred had been three years before when she was sixteen. She had just come from her morning bath. Her favorite nurse, Diana, had gotten her out of the tub and wrapped her in a bath sheet, but then Diana had been called away, probably to help one of Psyche's sisters, Iris or Lily who despite having their own slaves always needed to use Psyche's as well.

Psyche had not slept well the night before, worrying over the news that people were saying she was more beautiful than Venus. Wrapped in the bath sheet, she had gone back to her bed to lie down. Mostly dry, but still wet under her arms and between her thighs, so she had opened the sheet and begun to dry herself. That was the first time she had felt the presence.

"Are you there?" she said softly to her ceiling, chiding herself even as she spoke. It was pure foolishness, but for a moment she was certain that an invisible man was watching her. Though she knew no one was there, the idea of how a man would see her naked body roused her interest, and she went to her toilet table to get her mirror.

The silver handle of the mirror was shaped like a voluptuous maiden holding her arms in a "V". Between her outstretched palms was the reflective glass. Psyche felt the curve of the maiden's hips and the dip of her waist as she grasped the handle. Beneath her thumb, she could feel the nubs of the silver nipples. She raised the mirror to inspect her face.

Psyche had always looked this way—wide, blue eyes, fringed with dark lashes and framed by arched eyebrows. Her nose was fine, showing that she was the daughter of a king, and her lips were full. She committed the sin of hubris by thinking that it was true, she was lovely, but not, she thought quickly, as beautiful as Venus.

Taking the mirror back to her bed, she lay down, holding it above her breasts. They were pale and pert, and she tried to imagine how a man would see her.

"What will my husband be like?" she had asked the air. "I hope he's not much older than thirty…" Of course he would be rich and most likely royal. Was it too much to wish for him to be handsome and kind?

Holding the mirror over her belly, she inspected her narrow waist. "I hope he talks to me and values my mind. I wish the gods would bless me with love." Even as the words were uttered, she knew it was unlikely. But caught in the fantasy of an imaginary future husband, she held the mirror over her pubis, seeing the still slightly damp hair there, curling in little tufts the color of golden honey. She studied the whorls and spirals imagining a man touching her there.

Putting the mirror down, she looked up at the canopy. "I beg the goddess to forgive me. I do not want to anger her. I want love only." A tear slipped from her eye and she became annoyed with herself. Her moon time must be approaching. Why else would she act this way? Talking to herself, begging the ceiling, feeling as though someone unseen was there and then crying. She sat up and returned the mirror to the table.

"Princess," Diana had said, returning, "forgive me. Let me get you dressed."

And then the sensation was gone. The hair on her neck had returned to normal. She worried for a moment that she was going mad, but then quickly forgot about it.

Until it happened again, and again. Countless times over the last three years she had felt the same feeling of being watched by unseen eyes.

And now, here in the monster's palace, she felt the same sensation even more intensely. The hair on the back of her neck rose, as did all the hairs on her body, as if someone was breathing in her ear and slowly sliding his fingertip down her spine. She shivered, realizing her nipples had grown hard. The light blond hairs on her arms were standing up, and though she was not cold, it was as if she was waiting to be embraced and sheltered by another.

AFTER REFRESHING herself with food and drink, Psyche followed Adora up the stairs to her bedchamber. Wool rugs dyed indigo lay on the marble floor. The bed was carved of cedar wood with a fine canopy and matching curtains of heavy velvet. Fine dresses, *stola*, of every color awaited her and, on the dressing table, there were necklaces of gold, encrusted with jewels, next to vases brimming with roses and narcissus.

Instead of a window, the room let off to a wide marble balcony. Dusky rose-colored silk curtains fluttered in the breeze. Psyche stepped out into the open air to stare in awe at the trees and mountains that surrounded her. Never had she been so surrounded by nature, or so far from other people. There were no other villas or farms and, though it was idyllic, Psyche felt the heavy weight of solitude.

The estate where she was now to live was massive. From the balcony, she could see exquisitely designed fountains and statues in the garden. There was a pool of blue tile that would be delightful to swim in in the heat of summer. Different colored flowers dotted one garden. In a separate patch of earth, herbs and vegetables grew in neat rows. In the distance, she could make out at least two orchards. This much land required many slaves, yet she only saw the one.

"Would you like to bathe, mistress?" Adora asked when Psyche came back inside.

"Yes." A bath would be welcome.

Unseen servants had brought the water and filled a large iron tub adorned with detailed images of love making. Psyche stared, making out positions she had never seen before—a man and woman on their hands and knees, the man taking her from behind, her hand reaching back to him; a woman astride a man, her breasts cupped in his hands; a woman on her knees before a man, his member between her lips. Psyche gasped and looked away. She had never thought of such a thing. People often kissed each other hello, to think of a woman taking a man's shaft into her mouth and then later kissing a friend! Well, a proper lady would never do such a thing. Still the idea would not leave her mind.

She slid into the scented bath, ready to relax into the warm water. The tub held heat well. Too well, for the water was burning hot. She wondered suddenly if this was how she was to die but pushed the thought away. It seemed she was not to die at all. Her suffering would be to live. Images of the winged one, holding her in the sky, flitted through her mind. The memory of his skin against her own made her warm inside and out. Images of the positions that decorated the tub filled her mind... she astride him as he cupped her breasts, he taking her from behind, or... no, she must be blushing crimson now, just the thought of seeing his shaft, of touching it. Glancing at her arms, she saw they were pink, the color her face must be. Adora stroked her shoulder with a warm cloth, but Psyche yelped and pulled away.

"Mistress, I fear you have a sunburn."

At first the slave's words made no sense. Having spent most of her life indoors, Psyche did not really know what a sunburn was. But today her bare skin had been exposed to the sun, and so close. High up in the air, it seemed a miracle she had not been burned up.

Psyche endured the hot water while Adora washed and brushed her hair, scenting it with iris oil. Finally, her pink skin protesting the heat, she rose from the bath. When she stood, Adora gasped, staring at Psyche's backside.

The slave went to the bath table and held out a mirror. Gazing into the silvered glass, Psyche saw that her back was red except the places his arms had held her. Across her back was the imprint of the god's arm and on her left buttock, the shape of his hand; the fingers clearly outlined where he had held her to him.

The blood rushed to her face, but shame still failed to come with it. Instead, only the ghost memory of the pleasure of rubbing against him. She would gladly give herself to him in any of the ways imprinted on the tub. Where was her honor? Her upbringing had been better than this. She had behaved scandalously, wrapping her naked legs around a man, be he god or not.

A princess was meant to be chaste and pure, to keep her legs together even if it meant plunging into the sea. Perhaps it was a test and she had failed. Perhaps the goddess had decided sacrifice was too good for her and was even now thinking of a crueler punishment. Though Psyche could think of no crueler punishment than learning what love was only to be given to a monster.

Adora dressed her in an expensive *stola* made of blue silk from the east. The fabric was light, yet even the soft touch of the gown tormented her tender backside. Psyche put a red hand to her brow, thinking her face must be burned too; but it was cool, as if his gaze had sheltered her from the burning rays of the sun.

She had to stop this foolishness! This must be Venus's curse. Perhaps the God of Love had pricked her with his arrow after all. It would be a fitting punishment, though Psyche had not been the one to commit the crime. She had never wanted men to worship her as a goddess and forsake Venus's temple to praise her instead. When they said she was lovelier than the Goddess of Love and Beauty, she had denied it, begging her father to make an announcement that it wasn't true. Comparing her to the goddess was like writing her name in blood on a curse tablet.

But she was just a girl, a pawn, not a player. Her father had boasted of her beauty, trying to win her the richest suitors, hoping they would come from far and wide and make his kingdom by the sea famous. And, in the end, no one had asked to marry her. Her sisters, less comely, were easily wed, easily with child while Psyche was forgotten.

"Mistress," Adora said, breaking her reverie, "are you hungry? The food is ready. You must eat, for you are pale."

Psyche laughed. She was anything but pale. Now her beauty was indelibly marred. Her perfect, creamy skin, gone. Unsure of how a sunburn worked, she wondered if her skin would be pink on her arms, legs and backside, with his handprint on her buttocks forever. Would freckles and moles come so she looked like a peasant? That was all the goddess had really needed to do. One pot of boiling oil and Venus could have her revenge. Instead, the goddess had commanded her son to deliver Psyche to the monster. And Psyche had wrapped her thighs around him like a common whore and fallen in love.

She expected the monster to come to dinner. Instead, for the first time in her life, she dined alone, surprised by her favorite dish of chicken stuffed with young, soft-skinned almonds and olives. Simple foods were a pleasure after what was usually served in her father's palace—peacock tongues and roast suckling-pig, lambs cooked in mother's milk, course after course of excess. It was a relief to eat food that was not so rich and not to have to talk to anyone.

After dinner, she slept alone in the grand bed, dreaming of golden eyes, feeling herself rubbing against the winged one's abdomen as he flew her over the sea. As the sun rose, she awoke to birdsong. Adora helped her dress and led her to the dining room where she ate grapes, bursting with juice, succulent meat, and freshly baked bread. Invisible hands played music for her, but the music made her want to weep with loneliness, so she left the palace to walk in the garden.

It was a fine spring day. The fountains glittered, statues of satyrs and nymphs were frozen at play in the green grass. Butterflies flitted and birds sang. Narcissus, iris, lilies, and violets blossomed, their little buds turned toward the sun. It was charming, but it was nothing compared to his eyes.

CHAPTER 3

"I HAVE COME TO MAKE YOU MINE"

Adora found Psyche in the garden before the sun set. She had thought to stay and watch it. What else was there to do?

"Dinner is ready, mistress," Adora said "The kitchen has prepared a special meal for you tonight."

"Is he here? Has your master come?"

"No," Adora said, glancing down to the ground. "Not yet."

Psyche returned to the house and sat by herself at the huge marble table. The lack of dining companions accused her of her crimes. It was unknown to eat alone. Once was a novelty. Twice felt like a punishment.

Though she needed little, dish after dish was served, as if she were attending a wedding. First there were figs and cheese, followed by wild hyacinth bulbs soaked in honey, a known aphrodisiac, especially when accompanied by arugula and pine nuts. Then came lamb baked in rice, seasoned with spices from the far reaches of the Empire, and for dessert, honey pastries made with walnuts and orange, sprinkled with pepper to accompany the Chaldean wine, perfectly mixed with water.

But it was a lonely pleasure to dine alone, to have no one to discuss the food with, no hostess to compliment. How peculiar to not listen to the other guests tell stories. Music was played by invisible hands, but the notes seemed melancholy without other ears to hear. The wild hyacinth bulbs left her full of longing for companionship and sad to have no one to speak to.

When Adora came for her after dinner, the slave looked especially timid.

"Mistress, tonight my master comes. He bid me tell you that you must never look upon him. He, forgive me mistress, he instructed me to blindfold you and bind you to the bed."

Is this how I'm to be sacrificed, trussed up like a pig for slaughter? Psyche imagined the goddess's wicked smile. Surely this was Venus's revenge. Psyche drank her full cup of wine.

"Have you seen him, Adora?" Was he so hideous?

"No, mistress, he sends me his messages with the wind." The slave said nothing more.

Psyche's hand shook as she poured another cup of wine. She staggered a bit as she walked up the stairs but would happily have drunk more.

In the bedchamber, she used the pot and washed her face. Adora plaited her hair into six braids, as if Psyche was a bride. The slave removed her *stola* and rubbed almond oil on her body.

Psyche's arms were less pink, but the skin would never be the perfect pale it had been. When the monster saw her, would he think her beautiful, or see her only as a plaything to torment before he killed her?

Telling herself to be brave, Psyche lay on the bed and allowed Adora to bind her wrists to the top of the bed with white linen strips. Dread gripped her belly as the slave took her ankles and loosely tied one and then the other to the bottom bedposts. Adora tied a black piece of cloth over Psyche's eyes, covered her with a sheet, and left without saying a word.

Psyche lay there waiting to be devoured. Adora had left the lamps lit, and though Psyche could not see, the monster would be able to see all of her. She prayed, begging the goddesses, each one in turn, to have mercy on her, but she begged Venus twice.

As soon as she stopped whispering, she felt his presence. There was no smell, no sound, but there was a sudden shift in consciousness.

"Have you come to kill me?" she asked. It was not her place to speak first, but she could not wait another moment.

"No," he said, slowly pulling the sheet off her. "I have come to make you mine."

His voice was not that of a hissing snake or the deep baritone of a cave-dweller, the way she had always imagined a Cyclops or the Minotaur. His voice was gentle, cultured, educated. It was the voice of someone who would read Cicero or perhaps Apuleius.

He said no more, and she could feel his eyes on her body, taking in her full breasts and her golden hair, her small waist, her shapely arms and thighs. Men had once composed poems detailing her attributes. Those poems had led her here.

"Why am I bound? I am willing to do what is asked of me."

"I wanted you this way," he said simply. The confidence in his tone and the richness of his house made her realize he was a creature denied nothing. He gently touched the bindings on her wrists and the blindfold. "You are forbidden from seeing me. You must never look upon me. I want you to understand this above all else."

"But why?" she asked, knowing she was being impertinent. She had never thought she would not be able to see the monster.

His finger came quickly to her lips as if to silence her. "Too curious," he said. "Don't let it be your undoing."

She started at his sudden touch. The tip of his finger brushed her lower lip as he moved it to her jaw and slowly traced the line to her chin. He trailed his finger down to her neck, over her collarbone and to her chest until he came to her breast. She remembered pressing them against the winged one.

Is it you? His finger on her lips. Was it the god and not a monster? The thought of the winged one gave her comfort. She took strength from the memory of his eyes gazing into hers, of his hand pushing her harder against him. In the darkness, she let the memory of his hands mix with the touch of the unseen one.

He stroked her breasts tenderly, and she could not help but imagine how her breasts looked in this unknown creature's hands. His hands felt large and strong, she hoped he would not use them to hurt her. He ran the tips of his fingers over her nipples in circles, warming her slowly and thawing her terror.

The gentleness of his touch calmed her. She had expected his hands to be quick and hard upon her body, but the way his fingers caressed her made her relax and give in to the desire he was rousing in her. She surprised herself by thrusting her breasts forward and offering herself to him. He took her nipple into his mouth and sucked slowly, making her gasp. It felt almost as good as when the goddess had touched her, and the fear was just as strong.

The unknown creature lapped at her slowly, suckling one breast and then the other. His hair brushed her face and she thought he smelled like ambrosia and iron or perhaps blood, but she was distracted as he gently flicked his tongue over her nipple until she moaned. His hands came to her belly, running his finger down her midline to her honey hair. She squirmed against her bonds, fearing the pain of the rending of her flesh. But his finger gently stroked the bud of her womanhood which grew hard at his touch, remembering. She thought of the glistening she had left on the winged one, and knew this unseen man was making her glisten still as she grew slick with desire. His tongue trailed from her breast down to her belly. The sensation was so strange, so enticing. He suddenly thrust his tongue into her navel. Her hips jerked under him, her body already betraying her.

But she dreaded what was to happen next. All the stories her sisters had told her about the pain of the first time filled her mind. He would tear her inside and make her bleed they had said.

She would not be able to walk for days; he would dishonor her like a slave. But it already felt better than she had ever imagined. Perhaps it was just another lie her sisters had told her. But, no, she had been to enough weddings to know about the terrible pain women endured for men's pleasure. At her cousin's wedding the music had paused just as the bride screamed, begging her husband to stop. Her mother and aunts had made light of it, but Psyche had seen that they still remembered the terror of their first time. Her heart began to pound under his hand. He stopped.

"Do you fear me?" he asked.

"Only, only if you wish me to."

"No. I do not. I will not hurt you."

"But," she said before she could stop herself, "but you will." A few tears escaped, hidden by the blindfold. She felt the heat of shame burn in her face and her chest.

"You fear the breaking of your maidenhead."

"It is not only that… It is being bound this way… Let me give myself to you willingly, not trussed up like a captive—not like this, not with my legs bound…"

He moved off her abruptly. She had said too much and been impertinent, speaking first, asking questions. Women were beaten for less—one of her father's subjects had beaten his wife to death for drinking too much wine. Another had disfigured his wife for breaking a vase. Both the women's fathers had brought cases against the husbands, but here Psyche was alone.

Women were meant to keep quiet and obey. She chided herself for arguing with an unseen monster. He had been gentle, but now he would take her roughly, make her scream with pain, and then leave her bound to the bed. He could leave her here as long as he liked. Her father and brothers were far away. No one would come for her.

"I would rather have you of your own will, Psyche."

He touched one ankle and then the other, and the binds disappeared. Her legs were free.

"Thank you…." she said, feeling a surge of gratitude. "What should I call you?"

"Call me husband," he said, touching her again between her open legs. His hands reminding her to keep them spread.

"Husband." The word felt like honey on her lips, honey that contained a bit of the comb and a stinger as well. This was not how she had imagined her wedding, but two mornings ago she had thought she needed to be a maiden in order to be sacrificed to the monster. She remembered how Venus had touched her in the same place, pushing against the barrier. This man would break the barrier open and make her his wife.

Psyche tried to steel herself for the oncoming pain, but was distracted by his lips on her belly. His hands pushed her legs wider and the soft hair of his head nuzzled her inner thigh. It tickled and she squirmed until she felt a silken sensation unlike any other. The images from the tub floated behind her eyes, only instead of the woman taking the man, this unseen monster was putting his mouth to her, licking her opening.

She almost wished her legs were still bound so she had an excuse for allowing this. That a man would put his tongue in a place men were not even meant to look! He licked her gently, but she held herself taut, trying to resist.

She was shameless now. Yet his tongue, together with his hands on her thighs was too much. Her breath came fast though she tried to be quiet. On the brink of desire, she could not contain herself. She longed for him to take her, to make her his. She had lost all she was, and now she spread her legs wide open for him to lap at her.

"Make noise for me," he said. "I want to hear your pleasure."

She obeyed him quickly. All she wanted to do was cry out for him and beg for mercy, and for more.

She was panting with unknown passion, moaning like a small animal. This was what the goddess's touch had done to her and this unseen creature—her husband—was licking her like the waves of the sea. He stopped and slid his finger inside her. She could feel how wet he had made her as her body rose to his hand.

"You're ready now," he said.

His weight shifted onto her. He parted her thighs wider with his own, and she tensed, taut with fear.

"Psyche," he whispered, "trust me." He placed his palm over her heart, the warmth of it calmed her. "It will only hurt for a moment." Then his shaft, rock hard, was against her inner thigh. She wondered if he had done this often, but then he ran his member over her, teasing the part that had just begged him to come in, and she ceased thinking all together. Slowly, tenderly, he slid himself into her. Piercing pain came as his shaft sank into her opening. She forced herself to keep her legs spread and give herself to him. She moaned again, this time in distress.

"Here," he said. She felt the rounded flesh of his shoulder on her lips. "Bite me as hard as you like. I will bear the pain as well."

Again all her training was gone. A princess would have refused to open her mouth, choosing instead to suffer in silence. But Psyche parted her lips, licking his shoulder. She could smell the sun on his skin and another smell, like air, like feathers.

He plunged into her and she bit him as hard as she could, passing on the sting as he broke through her maidenhead. Though he thrust into her gently, she did not think she could endure it. She bit so as to not scream. No music would mask her cries.

And then as he moved gently against her, the sensation changed, the pain mixed with pleasure. Suddenly, the pain was not as important as him being there, inside her. Making what had only been hers his own. Sharing that sacred space with her permission.

She moaned and let go of his shoulder. He pushed himself into her deeper and when he pulled back, she longed for him to thrust into her again. She arched toward him, holding onto him with her legs, seeking to press as much as herself to him as she could. She moved against him on her own, overcome with the desire for him to take her completely, the ache only highlighting the pleasure she felt of having him inside her. Squeezing him tight with her thighs, she came into her pleasure fully, feeling her womb spasm as he spent himself inside her.

In the darkness, she saw the winged one's golden eyes, the goddess's wicked smile. She came back to herself. Her wrists were still tied to the bed. She was still blindfolded.

"Husband," she said, feeling the weight of the word on her tongue. *Husband.* She was married now.

"Yes?" he whispered in her ear.

"Did I bleed much?"

Through the blindfold the light shifted. He lifted the lamp above her. For a second she feared him dripping hot oil on her flesh.

"Not much," he said. "But enough to prove your innocence. I hope I did not hurt you too much, Psyche."

"It was worth the pain."

"I will untie you if you swear to never look on me and not to touch me. I want you to trust me, and I want to trust you. For there can be no love without trust. Promise me?"

She would promise him anything if he would come back and do that to her again. And perhaps it would be all right if she could just imagine him to be the winged one. Maybe he was a hideous beast on the outside, but in the dark, he was a kind lover.

"Yes," she said. "Only, I do not think I can promise not to touch you. I feel that I will yearn for you and…." She blushed. Her father would be mortified. He would whip her himself if he knew the things she had done since leaving home. "I… forgive me, husband. I have never said such things before. I will obey you as a wife should."

At his touch, her wrists were freed. She stretched her arms and pulled them to her sides, resisting the urge to sit up. He took her left wrist in his hands and slipped something cold and heavy onto it.

"Your wedding band," he said. "I wish I could have given you a more traditional wedding night, but I can at least give you this cuff."

Tears came to her eyes. She stroked the bracelet with her right hand, woven metal in a complicated design, silver or gold. She could feel two gems and wondered what they were—if their color and shape would give her a hint to what he was. She thought again about the weddings she had been to—the contracts, exchanges, vows, and agreements.

"But I have no dowry, husband."

"Your bride-price is all that you have lost and suffered for your beauty. That is all over now. I will care for you, Psyche, because I choose to, not because I have an agreement with your father. I seek nothing from him, and"—she thought she heard a smile in his voice—"I have no need of money."

"Let me give you this." She lifted her head and unclasped the golden necklace she had worn all along. "Please, husband," she said groping for his hand. "This is my only possession and I want you to have it."

He took her hand and the chain. "I will take this gladly, but it is not your only possession. You own everything in my house, now. And even naked with no jewels, you possess a great beauty." He caressed her face and extinguished the light.

"I will not keep you blindfolded, my love. I will come only in the dark. I only wanted to see you once, to glimpse your famed beauty said to be greater than Venus."

"Please, do not say that. It is not true. I am only a mortal trembling before the gods. My beauty has been a curse since it has not brought me love." She smiled, wanting to add *until now*, but she was too embarrassed to say the words out loud, so she said instead, "You know about me, yet I know nothing of you, except you have been kind to me this night."

She could not tell, but it sounded as though he laughed.

"No one has called me kind before—cruel, I have been called many times, and heartless, merciless, unpredictable, and wrathful. Fathers advise their sons to avoid me at all costs, but no one can escape me once I set my sights on them—even the gods fear me..." He spoke almost as if to himself. "I am a creature cursed with a power I am only now beginning to understand... I am unlovable."

"No," she said. "You are no longer that." She touched his hand and quickly pulled away. The back of his hand felt normal and she knew his palms and fingers were those of a man, and the other parts of his body that had touched her own—his shoulder, his belly, his thighs felt like a well-muscled man, not a hairy beast or a scaled monster.

"Forgive me, husband. I have never been so forward or so disobedient. I only want to tell you that it does not matter to me what others say of you. You could have done anything with me." Her voice quivered. She stroked the wedding band on her wrist, the solid weight of it giving her strength. "But you chose to treat me well, to be kind to me—to, to give me pleasure when you could have easily only given me pain... But perhaps you were right to bind me to the bed, for I cannot promise to not touch you in moments of passion. If you wish to bind my wrists, I will not refuse."

He did laugh then. It was a dry sound like the wind in the leaves in winter. He took her cold hand and enveloped it in his two larger ones.

"You desire to touch me, though I am a monster? I had thought tying you to the bed would be the only way I could have you. It seems you have already taught me more than I have learned in centuries." He brought the back of her hand to his lips and kissed it. "I will permit you to touch me in passion, Psyche, only not my face or back. I have scars there that shame me, and I would not want you to feel them. I mean this, now. You must obey me."

She was aware of the heat of her own back, suddenly grateful he had not commented on her pink arms, that he had not seen her backside and the imprint of the hand. Fear and confusion overcame her. She must forget the winged one. If it were he, he did not want to be known. If her husband was not the god, but a monster, then she betrayed his kindness by thinking of another. And why should she think of the other when she was with this one now, a shadow husband who had been so tender.

She wanted to argue that she did not care if he was scarred, for she was willing to love him for all that he was, but she knew better than to say more. He had already given her more freedom than he had intended.

Finding his shoulder, she brushed her lips against it, feeling the indentation her teeth had left there and kissed it gently. "I will obey you, husband, I swear on my soul."

CHAPTER 4

INJECTING VENOM

The next morning Psyche awoke in the grand bed alone. With the velvet curtains closed, it was completely dark though birdsong told her the sun had risen. She imagined parting the curtains and catching a glimpse of her husband. In her mind, he was the winged one, and she desired only to behold his beauty. But even before she opened the curtain, she knew he was gone.

The room was filled with the golden glow of a countryside morning. Slivers of sunlight reflected off her wrist and she held it out to examine her wedding band. Pure gold with silver and gold threads entwined to make a pattern. She rotated her wrist to find it was a snake eating its own tail; its eyes green with emeralds. It was the most exquisite wedding band she had ever seen.

She turned the bracelet to the side to unlatch the snakehead and examine it more carefully, but she could find no place to open it. She had never seen a piece of jewelry like this and had no idea how to take it off. For a moment she imagined it had been made by the God of the Forge, Vulcan—Venus's husband, that somehow the bracelet was enchanted and would keep her chained in the monster's palace. And then, as she gave into foolishness, she wondered if her husband was telling her with this gift that he was a serpent.

But she was thinking like a child. Surely the God of the Forge had not made her wedding band. Just because it was well-crafted did not make it enchanted. And, really, there was no need for her to take it off. Snake bracelets and rings were popular, a symbol of long life, surely that was all it meant.

She stood up and stretched, admiring the grandeur of her bedchamber. The dusky rose curtains fluttered in the gentle breeze, and smells of a spring morning drifted in. Even though the doors to the balcony had been open all night, there were no mosquitos or fleas; not even a fly had bothered her since she had arrived. Wrapping herself in a wool shawl, she stepped onto the balcony, to gaze upon her husband's land.

Psyche had always hoped to marry a handsome man, but now she reflected that good-looking men were often cruel. Granted whatever they asked, they expected all and did not learn kindness. She thought of her brothers, handsome, rich, and spoiled. Her sisters' husbands were even worse. They had seemed the pinnacle of male beauty, but their hearts were cold. Perhaps it was better to have a hideous monster who was loving in the dark, than a man who was beautiful in the day and cruel at night.

When she reentered the room, she saw the bloodstain on the sheet. If she had been at home, the women would have come to her chamber the morning after the wedding, bringing bread, honey, and beer. While her husband ate with the men, the women would have examined the sheet, commenting on the blood, the shape and size of the stain. They would divine what it meant for her future and how many children she would have. They would have recounted their own wedding nights, some with happier memories than others, but they would have come together as women to celebrate this.

Psyche stared at the sheet alone, thinking of her sisters. She imagined how Iris would say in her superior way that with time,

Psyche might find pleasure with her husband. Lily would add that if Psyche were lucky, she would learn to love him. And then they would see her blush. They would guess but not believe her happiness, and their hearts would swell with jealousy. Psyche laughed out loud in the empty room. The bright curtains fluttered, the statues watched her in silence.

Adora came with bread and figs. Psyche ate and took a leisurely bath. When it came time to dress, she examined her new wardrobe. There were so many exquisite dresses, in a variety of fabrics; many were even woven with gold thread. On this morning, she decided on a light pink linen gown. Adora dressed her and did her hair. Psyche stared at herself in the mirror. She was still beautiful, but who would see her?

Yet she would not be idle. There was a loom and wool, finer than any she had seen. She had never been very good at weaving. Perhaps this was her chance to improve. But it did not take long until frustration overtook her. The wool became entangled and she gave up.

The cool of the garden would distract her. She walked about. Perhaps she could recognize some of the herbs. She tried in vain to recall which ones could help a woman conceive a child. Her nurse had told her these things, but she had failed to listen, thinking Diana would come with her if she ever got married.

Giving up on the herb garden, Psyche went to admire the statues. Amidst the greenery and flowers were a nymph, a satyr, a discus thrower, and a pair of lovers. They were exquisitely wrought of bronze, but they did not make good companions.

She glanced up at the sun. It was much too high in the sky. She understood then how it would be. This glorious palace would be a gilded cage of solitude. Her days were to pass in suspended boredom, waiting for him.

But though every day was spent in longing, every night as the sun set and the lamps were lit by invisible servants, her heartbeat quickened with excitement. She ate early and bathed, then once it was completely dark, she would shut the curtains of the balcony, always leaving the door open. After climbing into bed naked, she would extinguish the lamp and close the bed curtains. Soon after, he would come for her and teach her about pleasure and love.

Despite the happiness of her nights, each day upon awakening she was filled with loneliness. She longed for her husband, for an intelligent voice, for any distraction. Psyche had never realized that solitude could be a prison. All the entertainment she had taken for granted, the traveling bards, the jugglers, and acrobats, even the blood sport she had detested and the gossip she had disdained before would have been welcome now. Just hearing the voices of others in animated conversation would have made her feel less lonely. She would even like to see her sisters.

In her solitude, she tormented herself with one question—was her shadow husband the god who had brought her here? Did she love him more intensely or was she betraying him? At times she was sure he was the winged one. It was as if she knew her unseen husband, understood him the same way she had when she looked into the winged one's golden eyes. But how could she know his mind without knowing what he looked like?

When he came to her in the darkness, he was at first ravenous with passion, which he quickly kindled in her. The desire she had for him was a shock, and she wished desperately to ask another woman if this was normal. As soon as she was with him, she thought of nothing else but pleasing him and herself, for it was a delight just to hear his voice and feel his skin against her own. Later they talked, sometimes all night. On more than one occasion, he left abruptly, having lost track of time, but desperate to leave before the first light of dawn.

It was easy to discover what they had in common. They had both been celebrated among their people, though it was only with each other in the dark that they were truly loved.

Even their own parents had kept them at arms' length. Her striking beauty had set her apart, and his power had kept anyone from getting too close. But together they were able to speak of all manner of things. It was oddly liberating speaking the truth in the dark to the husband she had never seen. After two months, Psyche felt she could say anything to her shadow husband, so she finally confessed what she had thought from the first night.

"Husband, I do not believe you are a monster." She held his hand in her own. Though their desire had been satiated for the time being, their bodies continued to touch.

"But I am, Psyche. You are the only one who does not think it so."

"How are you a monster?" Her voice was little more than a whisper. She was not supposed to ask.

"I was born with a terrible power that brings both mortals and gods to their knees. No one, not even Jupiter, can stop me." His voice sounded raw. "I, I can if I so desire it, inject venom that causes folly or madness."

She wondered if he meant his arrows, that his venom was heartbreak. What would happen if she asked him if he was the God of Love? What if he really was a creature with great fangs that poisoned gods and men for fun? Would he grow angry and devour her?

So instead she asked, "Why do you do it, husband?"

"When I was a child, I thrived on the attention. The gods themselves ingratiated themselves to me to do their bidding. The pain I caused was just a wildly amusing game to me. As I grew, I realized that these creatures I played with were not just toys." His voice broke. It sounded as if he were trying not to cry.

"In the past, I laughed at the foolish sorrows of mortals. I delighted in the tears I caused them to shed, in the blood I caused to spill. But after I saw you, my love, something changed." He stroked her cheek in the darkness. "Many have died from my venom, more live on with the wounds I inflicted. I once reveled in their suffering, but now it sickens me to think of what I have done, and what I will do again. Yet I cannot help myself. I know in the future, perhaps tomorrow, perhaps next month, I will see some hapless mortal and without thinking I will strike. The thought that I could have done this to you torments me."

There were tears in his voice. Without thinking, she reached out to wipe his cheeks, but he sensed her hand above his face and gripped her wrist hard, pinching the skin between her wedding bracelet and his hand.

"What are you doing?" he growled. "You must never touch my face. You will betray me, Psyche! I know you will. Yet I've given you my heart and cannot take it back."

"Husband, please, I know—"

He let go of her wrist and placed his finger roughly on her lips.

"If you break your promise to me, I will be forced to leave you. Don't make me punish you, Psyche."

She had only wanted to dry his tears, but now she shed her own. It was unbearable to think of life without him. The thought was like a knife in her heart, giving her a taste of the fear of his venom. Being lonely all day was a delight compared to the thought of never seeing him again.

He pulled her to him, letting her tears fall on his neck. His smell of ambrosia, metal, and a slight hint of leather filled her with yearning. She clung to his torso as he sank his fingers into her hair. Tentatively, she put her hand on his chest, the muscles on the right more defined than the left, like an archer.

"You can touch me," he said, "but never can you see my face, Psyche, my soul. Never do I want you to know how much of a monster I truly am."

AFTER THE TURNING of four moons with no one to talk to during the day, she feared she would go mad. No matter how late she rose, the sun was always too high in the sky, the time the sun would set too far away. Sometimes madness would overcome her, and she'd think perhaps he could blind her and then they could spend their days together.

She missed Diana desperately. Her old nurse had been Psyche's sole companion during the last three years when no man sought her. In addition to entertaining Psyche with wondrous tales from Greece and other parts of the Empire, Diana always knew how to soothe her. The loneliness would be bearable if the old woman were there. Most importantly, she could ask Diana all the questions she didn't dare ask her husband.

Psyche felt a pang, not just for Diana, but for her mother and father, the slaves and retainers she had grown up with. They all thought her dead, yet she was alive, happily married, with more riches than she had ever imagined.

Everyone should know. How pleased they would be that she lived! Her mother had begged the priest of Apollo not to take their daughter's life. Her father had tried to bribe him. But the oracle had made it clear that Psyche was to be left on the beach. If only they knew she was still alive. Guilt overtook her suddenly that she had not tried to send a message sooner.

When her husband came that night, he seemed to know immediately that something was amiss.

"My soul, what troubles you?"

"Husband," she said, still relishing the sound of the word in her mouth. "I miss you so during the day. I have no one to talk to. My family thinks I am dead. I must see them. Please, is there no way I can go to them?"

"No, Psyche. The Goddess of Love would be furious. She wants you miserable. It would not do for you to return, alive and shining with happiness."

Suddenly there was a pain in her throat of unshed tears and a tightness in her chest. It was as if she were a small child. She had asked for something, he said no, and now she wanted to cry. She lay still in the dark, angry with herself, angry with him. Were they having a fight? Her thoughts turned to her elder sister Iris flinging pottery at her husband in a rage over the most recent pregnant slave, and her elder brother who had not spoken to his wife in years. He only went to her in the dark and took his need of her without a word. Were all marriages doomed to end in sorrow?

"Can you bring them here?" she asked. Perhaps even the winged one could bring them. If she heard his voice, she would know for sure.

"No, my soul. I must not."

"But they think I'm dead. They think you've eaten me."

"No," he said again. "It is unwise."

"Yes, husband." She gave up and let the foolish tears come. He kissed her and she lay still, letting him touch her, but not returning his affection.

She tried not to sulk the next night, to accept his decision as a good wife would, but a deep sense of loneliness had crept into her soul. A kind, loving husband was all she had thought she wanted, but now that she had him, the rich life he gave her was not enough. She would gladly exchange the gilded plates, the shimmering jewels, the silken dresses for Diana, or even to see her sisters Lily and Iris again. She loved her shadow husband and had grown used to being with him in the dark, but there were things she wished to discuss, things she could only talk about with another woman.

On the tenth night after he had denied her request, he came later than usual. Perhaps she had angered him with her sorrow. What if he had grown tired of her? Love was nothing if not fickle. What if he was not the God of Love, but a real monster and he had somehow found out that she pined for the winged one? She resisted the urge to pace the room. He would be angry if he came in and she was not in the bed waiting for him.

A soft sound on the wind let her know he had come. He parted the curtain, always too quickly for her to see even his silhouette, and was beside her.

"Husband," she said gladly, sitting up in the darkness.

"My soul." He took her hand, stroking it with his fingers and speaking slowly. "Psyche, you are teaching me much about love. I have discovered that my happiness now depends on your own. My love for you has turned me into a fool, but I cannot bear your sorrow. Though I fear it will be our undoing, I have decided to allow your sisters to come visit you. I will arrange for it on the morrow."

"Oh!" she cried, restraining herself from touching his face with her lips as she wanted to. Instead, she touched his shoulder, the place she had bitten him the first time.

Truly, she thought, if he knew her so well, he would guess that she wanted Diana or her mother to come instead of her sisters. But he had made such a kind gesture to have changed his mind on this. She could not ask him for something different.

He lay down, pulling her with him onto the bed. She was suddenly giddy and impassioned, wanting to have him in a way she never had before. Her mouth suddenly seemed to have a will of its own, and she licked his nipple. He put his hands in her hair and pulled slightly, encouraging her. She moved down, opening her lips and running her tongue along his taut abdomen. It was like silk under her tongue and she slowly licked his belly, teasing him until he moaned with desire. His manhood brushed her cheek, standing erect, awaiting her attention.

The image from the bathtub flashed through her mind, a woman on her knees taking a man in her mouth. Just a short time ago, this act, this thing she now desired to do as much as he desired her to do it, had been unimaginable. But this man was her husband, and she wanted to make him moan for her.

She nuzzled the pointed tip and licked him tentatively. He pulled at her hair, guiding her head over him and inserting himself in her mouth. He gasped as she enveloped him, sucking on him as though his member were a finger dipped in honey.

She had never imagined controlling a man this way. He

seemed to be struggling with himself as she began to move her head up and down on him. He tilted his pelvis and she took him more fully, then pulled back and ran her tongue over his shaft. She stroked his strong thighs with her fingers, gently caressing his tight sac. He was on the brink, and she took him fully into her mouth to the opening of her throat. Would his seed be divine? Sweet like a god's, or vile and swimming with demons like a monster's?

She pulled back for a moment, licking the tip and tasting a sweet, salty fluid. But before she could envelope him again, he pulled her off him and flipped her, so she was underneath him and he astride her. His organ, wet from her mouth, teased at her opening. She was slick with desire for him, and he slipped himself inside her, making her gasp.

"Psyche," he said, thrusting against her, "I fear I love you too much."

"No," she said, pushing against him. She entwined her legs with his and cupped his buttocks with her hands. "Love is never too much."

THE NEXT DAY she rose early. Of course he was gone. She often imagined what it would be like to have a husband in bed in the morning, to admire while sleeping. He would look like the winged one. His fine brown hair, slightly wild, tousled with sleep. She would watch the light play on his wings and his strong shoulders. Then they would break bread together; eat figs, fresh from their tree. In the garden he would pick flowers for her as they lay in the shade enjoying the music of the fountain. There would be no need to speak because all they need do was look in each other's eyes. His gold and all knowing, hers… Oh, she must stop! She did not have that husband. She had a shadow husband who loved her too much.

Rising from bed, she realized that today she had something to do. She bathed quickly. There had been more than enough long leisurely baths. After some thought, she decided on the green silk *stola* and a golden necklace with a large emerald which would bring out the color of her eyes.

Adora did a fair job on her hair though not as good as the hairdresser slave Psyche's mother had kept. She could replicate the latest styles perfectly. Here, cut off from the world, Psyche did not know the most recent fashion. There was no time to have her hair curled, so she had Adora braid it and put it up, using a green ribbon as a hairband.

After examining her face in the mirror, she decided to forego makeup. She had rarely worn any at home, and she did not want her sisters to think she had tried too hard. They were family after all.

She strode out of the palace, eager to see her sisters. After walking through the trees, she found the spot where the winged one had brought her. Adora came with fruit, bread, and a blanket, for the days were turning cold.

Had time always moved this slowly? She did not think it had, but every moment seemed to take three times as long as it had before.

There in the sky, she saw a speck. It was a bird. Three specks later something seemed to come toward her. Her heart leapt to her throat. Two people flew through the sky—a winged man carrying a woman. She stood waiting, forcing herself to stay calm.

A good wife would focus on the woman. One of her sisters. She should rejoice to see her kin, but all she could do was track the movements of the winged man.

Even before she could make out his features, she knew it was not him. This man was bronze-skinned but with silver hair and wings shining in the sun. His frame was different, too, wispy and slight. His skin was both momentarily transparent and solid. The woman's red hair shone in the sun—her eldest sister Iris. The winged god held her in his arms like a mother holds an infant to present to its father. If only her winged one had held Psyche like that, everything would have been different.

The silver-haired god landed and folded back his wings.

"Psyche!" Iris said, unsteady on her legs. The one who held her put an arm out to keep her from falling. Iris glared at him.

"What is this?" Iris asked. She had never liked surprises.

"Sister," Psyche said, showing the proper respect to her elder. Then she turned to the man who she knew was not a man at all.

"Thank you," she said, "my lord…"

"I am Zephyr, God of the West Wind."

His eyes were the color of the sky and Psyche made the mistake of staring a moment too long. She felt as if she were flying on the wind. Though the god before her appeared gentle, she could feel the quiet strength of his power. Iris's eyes had narrowed a bit, but she caught herself and smiled.

"Little sister, I am so relieved to see that you are alive. We mourned you for dead until today."

"Princess Psyche," Zephyr said, "I will bring your second sister."

"Thank you, Lord Zephyr." She was unable to resist glancing into his eyes and savoring the moment of feeling she was flying again. He lifted off the ground, propelled by the wind and, once airborne, spread his wings toward the direction from which he came.

She turned back to Iris. "Sister, let me welcome you into my home and offer you food and drink."

Iris followed her to the palace and Adora brought wine, pastries, and fruit. Once Psyche was assured Iris was comfortable, she went to wait for Lily.

Both Iris and Lily were striking—Iris's wild, red hair and blue eyes had brought her many suitors. Lily was lithe and pale with green, almost yellow, eyes and a flowing mane of blond hair.

They were both stunning, but it was Psyche the people chose to worship.

Yet while Psyche's beauty was famed throughout the land, no king or prince came forth to ask for her to be his wife. Iris and Lily were quickly married to princes in neighboring kingdoms. Psyche had heard the happy news of the children they had borne their husbands, but she had not seen her sisters in years.

Psyche gazed up into the sky and saw Zephyr descending, gliding down to where she stood. Wild-eyed, Lily clutched Zephyr's neck tightly. But when she saw Psyche, she underwent a change, composing her face and straightening her back.

"Little sister," Lily said, as Zephyr set her down, "look at you! Beautiful as ever!" Lily was pale, but she was never one to show surprise, so she acted as if it were nothing, to be flown through the air and brought to a palace to see the sister she had thought dead.

"Welcome to my home, elder, you too are looking well." In truth Lily appeared haggard. There were new lines around her eyes. The white powder she wore had found its way into the creases, highlighting them instead of hiding them. Her lipstick was far too bright and the blush made her look foolish. Psyche almost wondered if the slave who had done Lily's hair and makeup had made her look garish on purpose.

The two sisters gazed at each other a moment. Psyche wished she had brought Adora to lead Lily into the house, for it was Zephyr she longed to speak to.

"I thank you for your assistance, Lord of the West Wind. Is there anything I can offer you?"

"That is kind, princess, but I have all I need."

She could not help but look into his eyes. The shade of blue seemed to be in a constant state of transformation, not as light blue as the sky at midday, not as dark as the deep sea, not as gray as an approaching storm, yet a combination of all these.

Psyche felt herself soar with him through the skies and, for a moment, she wished only to fly away with him. It was not love, nothing like she had felt with the winged god or her husband, only a desire for freedom.

"May I ask, Lord Zephyr, if you have known my husband long?"

"Yes, since he was a child."

"And… is he as bad as they say?"

Zephyr's blue eyes clouded for a moment and Psyche felt the air around him surge with his power. The wind was ready to blow, waiting for his command.

"He is so much worse, princess. I pray to the gods you never have to find out how terrible he is. If you need me—when you want your sisters returned to their homes, just call out on a breeze or have your slave send a message." Zephyr gave her a slight bow and flew straight up into the air where he rode a current and floated out of sight.

Psyche regretted that Lily had heard, but it had been her only chance to talk to a being who knew her husband. Lily's green-yellow eyes grew wide with interest.

"Sweet girl," she said, "I am so happy to find you alive." Lily embraced her, but Psyche could see through her almost as clearly as the wind.

Psyche brought Lily to the palace, telling herself she was glad to see her and Iris. Now that they were grown, married women, it would be different. But she could sense her sisters' jealousy as they took in all the fine things her husband had given her.

They sat in the garden, waiting for dinner. Psyche watched her sisters eye the statues and the fountains amid the flowers still in bloom in late summer.

"Your husband's gardeners are so skilled," Lily said. "How lucky you are to have wed such a rich man."

"When will he be home?" Iris asked.

"Oh, I'm afraid he's hunting today."

"Tell us all about him," Lily said.

"What does he hunt?" Iris asked.

"Deer," Psyche said. She had thought it all out, but she had forgotten how Iris could always get the truth from her. If Psyche ever had a secret, Iris always knew, the same way a cat found a wounded bird.

"What kind of deer?" Iris asked, then added, "I was so looking forward to meeting him—this husband of yours, little sister. How we mourned when we heard you had been sacrificed to a terrible monster. We rejoice to see you alive and beautiful. Don't we, Lily?"

"Oh, yes," Lily added, staring at Psyche's gown.

"You know, dear sister," Iris said, taking her hand, "if you have any troubles you can tell us. We will help you. Your husband, is he… does he treat you well?"

"Yes," Psyche said brightening. "He's wonderful. I never imagined such a husband. He gives me whatever I desire before I even know what it is! He has never been unkind or beaten me. I did not know such a man could possibly exist!"

"And is he," Iris asked, "a man, or is he, something else?"

Psyche's happiness melted away. There was no escaping telling them. She looked down and noticed how worn their sandals were in comparison to her own.

"The truth is," she said softly, "I do not know. He has forbidden me from seeing him in the light."

"So he is the monster," Lily said, a gleam in her yellow eyes. Psyche had not been devoured, but she had not wed a mortal.

"He does not act like a monster."

"Not yet" Iris said. "But he will. All men are monsters eventually. Now he enjoys your innocence but as time goes on, he will tire of you. Men always do."

"Perhaps," Lily added, "this is part of the goddess's punishment, to make you love a monster and then let you see him." She smiled. "He will be a hideous beast, but you will love him still.

Then everyone will hear of how the greatest beauty gave her heart to the ugliest creature!"

Psyche knew this game. She was five years old again, tricked into giving her favorite doll to her sisters, who threw it in the fire. She was nine years old, still wanting them to like her, fooled into letting Lily "borrow" her most beautiful dress while Psyche wore a faded gown to the festival. Tears burned her eyes, but she would not let them fall. She would not let her sisters bully her any longer!

"If that is how the goddess wants to punish me, I will bear it. For I know something now. I have learned about love, and I know what it is. If my husband is a monster, I will love him still. He is kind and, even in the darkness, given half the time with him in the night as most couples have in the day, it is still more than most get in a lifetime!" She was only trying not to cry, but she could see that her words were like knives to her sisters.

Psyche had always been able to divine the feelings of others, but since the goddess had touched her, this sense had been heightened. As clearly as if their actions were real, she felt Iris's desire to slap her and Lily's secret fantasy of stabbing her through the heart. Her sisters looked at each other with sharp eyes. They would make Psyche pay, and there was no one here to stop them. But then the hair on the back of her neck rose and she could feel the presence of another. Was it him? The winged one, her husband, or someone else?

Suddenly Adora came. "Mistress, the feast is ready."

The three princesses rose and followed Adora into the dining room. Psyche trembled and wondered if Adora had just saved her life.

SITTING AT THE TABLE, with plates of roasted lamb, figs, bread, and a carafe of wine, Lily and Iris exchanged gossip. They made sure Psyche's cup was never empty as they laughed at the foibles and misfortunes of those they had grown up with.

"So, little sister," Lily said, "when will you bear your secret husband a child? Perhaps then you will know what kind of man he is."

"Yes," Iris added, "when you see the serpent's head emerge from between your thighs!" Both sisters laughed.

As usual they knew exactly how to torment Psyche. This was what she yearned to discuss with them.

"How long did it take you to get with child?" she asked her sisters.

"I was wed for only one month," Iris said. "It took you much longer, didn't it, Lily?"

"Six months. But I was glad of it since I ended up having twins."

Psyche sighed to herself and drank her wine. She had forgotten how they could make anything a competition.

"And I might have a third in my belly right now," Iris said. "Little Psyche, it shouldn't take that long if you're doing every-thing right. If you want a baby, you must not take any pleasure in it. They say if you enjoy it too much, your fluids will wash his seed out." She poured more wine in Psyche's cup.

"How did you know when you were with child the first time?" Psyche asked.

Her sisters grinned at each other.

"How long has it been since you bled?" Iris asked.

"More than a month, but not yet two." Psyche said, wishing her mother had come instead.

"Are your breasts tender?" Iris asked.

"Yes."

"And are you tired?" Lily asked.

"Perhaps. I sleep a lot..."

"Oh, this is wonderful!" Lily said.

"Yes," Iris added. "But it must be so strange to have never seen your husband! I would go mad with curiosity. I think I might light a lamp one night while he slept, just to see. Especially if his child is lodging in your womb, little sister."

"But you must be careful not to lose it. That can happen if you displease the gods."

"Yes," Iris said, "you must be very careful now. If you anger any of the goddesses, they will make you sick every day of the pregnancy. Although, we already know how Venus hates you. If she wishes, she can kill the baby in your womb or make it deformed, so you have a monster growing inside you. Oh, so pale, little sister. Don't worry, just go to a temple of Diana and sacrifice to her—that is if you can get off this mountain—maybe your husband can have his friend the wind carry you there—if you don't grow too heavy for him." She snickered, pouring herself and Psyche more wine.

Psyche looked away from her sisters into her grand house. She had everything a woman could want. Why was it not enough?

"Lily," Iris said brightly, "have you heard the stories of the monstrous serpent that roams the nearby hills? They say he comes in the day while the men are away with the sheep. He hypnotizes the women with his eyes and then devours the children."

"Yes!" Lily said, her yellow eyes glowing. "The Day Killer they call him. I heard it said that he has come because one of the gods is angry. They are not sure which, perhaps Juno or Venus— you know how wrathful she can be. I'm glad I never roused her ire."

Psyche was fairly sure they were lying. But she was still their little sister, wanting to believe them, and she had been away from the world for so long.

"What if your husband is this creature?" Iris asked as if just thinking of it.

"That's not possible," Psyche said. "He has the body of a man, not a snake. I have never seen him, but I have felt him." Thinking of all they had done in the dark, heat came into her cheeks.

"Then you've felt the snake between his legs!" Lily said cackling, making Psyche blush more.

"Oh, little Psyche, how you've grown!" Iris said. "But, you know, he could still be a monster. These creatures can change their shape when they're awake. He can feel like a man, but still not be one. Perhaps that is why he won't let you see him. Maybe he can hold the shape of a man, but not have the proper color. In his sleep, his natural shape will return. You need only to wait until he sleeps, then light a lamp and look."

"Yes," Lily said. "And if he is a monster, take a knife and kill him. Then you will be free of this." She gestured at the dining room, attempting to eye the mosaics and golden statues with disdain.

Psyche felt the blood drain from her face. The thought of betraying her husband, of killing him! The kind one who had been so gentle with her, repaying him with treachery! Never. She wanted to scream at her sisters to leave. They were not welcome in her home any longer. But they were still her elders. She dared not insult them.

She rose on unsteady feet. "Forgive me. I am suddenly unwell. I must retire to my rooms. Rest here. My servant will call Lord Zephyr. She will tell you when he comes, and he will take you home."

"Oh no, dear Psyche, we will tend to you!" Iris rose and Lily too. They would follow her to her room.

"No," Psyche said. "The only cure for this ailment is being alone." She stepped away from them towards the marble staircase. But they followed, like hounds after a wounded deer. She knew what would happen. Feigning concern for her health, they would refuse to leave, polluting her mind and her house.

Psyche turned and held her ground, mustering her strength. "I am so grateful that you came, sisters. Please, tell mother and father I am safe and well—that they need not worry for me, and... let me give you both a token of my gratitude. Take anything you want from this room before you leave."

It was like throwing a dog a bone. Both her sisters turned away from her, false concern gone as they scanned the room for portable treasure. Psyche turned and ran up the stairs, hoping for Zephyr's sake they took only what they could manage.

In her room, with the beautiful carpets and the exquisite bed, she wept bitter tears. Iris and Lily were vipers. She had thought she was miserable because she was lonely, but in truth she had always been lonely. Now at least at night, he came. He understood her in the darkness as no one understood her in the light.

She would accept her husband—whatever he was. God or monster, she loved him for how he treated her. From the moment the goddess touched her, though it had been in hatred, she had begun learning about love. When the winged one flew her over the sea, she discovered the desire of the flesh, and when her husband took her maidenhead, she had learned how deeply entwined pain and pleasure were. And now she tried to learn about fidelity.

But the wine sang its own song to her. *Why does your husband forbid you from seeing him? He has seen you completely and you have never seen him at all. It is not right. You should see him just once.* And the question that plagued her came again. Were her shadow husband and the winged one the same? She must know!

What is wrong with a little peek? And if you do carry his child, you must know what kind of child it is to be, divine or monstrous? And perhaps, do get a knife, for if he is a monster, you might not want to live with that knowledge.

His touch in the darkness woke her. She was still fully dressed, her face sticky with tears. Her head ached though the wine was still in her blood, still singing its song.

"What happened, my soul?" he asked gently. He expected her to be naked in bed, waiting for him as she was every night.

"Oh, husband! You were right. It was a mistake to see my sisters. They despise me as they always have; and Venus, the goddess I wanted to please the most, hates me. Everyone loves or hates me for my beauty, not for who I am on the inside."

He wiped her tears away. "That is why I come to you in the dark, Psyche. It is true you were given to me because of your beauty. Indeed, it drew me to you, but now, I have come to love your soul." He touched her breast through the cloth. "In this room, in the darkness, we can speak the truth. You love me even though others fear me. You love me without knowing who I am."

"But how I can I love you that way?" she asked in anguish. "I want to love you completely, not only in the dark. Please, let me...."

He clamped his hand over her mouth roughly.

"Don't ask me. You cannot know."

His words renewed her tears, which flowed over his hand. He lifted his hand from her mouth and wiped the tears from her cheeks. Kissing her neck, he whispered in her ear. "Psyche, my child grows in your womb. If you keep faith with me, she will be divine."

Joy surged through her. She found his lips and kissed them, reveling in the softness of his skin. Though he had forbidden her from touching his face, she needed this.

"You disobey me, Psyche, yet I do not fault you for this. I want your mouth on mine as much as you want the same." He delved his tongue between her lips.

She moaned at the pleasure of it and kissed him back. He usually touched her gently, but tonight he seemed unsatisfied with caresses. His hands were suddenly rough on her shoulders, pushing her onto her back. His fingers brushed her nipples as he gripped the delicate fabric of her *stola*. She arched toward him and he rent the fabric down the middle baring her to the waist.

"Husband," she whispered in surprise.

He gripped her naked breasts, kissing her throat savagely.

"You belong to me Psyche, not your sisters, not the goddess, but to me. You are mine." His hands were hot upon her, his need urgent as he straddled her. She was not prepared when he parted her thighs with his knees and thrust himself inside her.

She gasped, shocked by the sudden pain. He had never taken her like this before. His mouth was hungry for her and he moved down to her breast, taking her nipple and suckling it hard. She put her hands on his shoulders, trying to calm his need, but his hands came up and held her wrists at her sides.

"Don't touch my back," he growled, taking her other nipple with the same ferocity. She cried out and he thrust into her deeper. *All men are monsters eventually.* Iris's words floated through her mind as he quickly took his need with her.

He shuddered into her and released her hands, rolling next to her. She wanted to cry, but did not. He was her husband. It was his right. She told herself it was a wonder that this was the first time he had not brought her pleasure. She had wanted to ask her sisters how often they enjoyed being with their husbands. But even without knowing what happened to other women, she knew she was lucky. Even if tonight had been different.

"Psyche," he said, softly, the smallest hint of regret in his voice. "I just needed you… Are you all right?"

"Yes, husband."

"Forgive me for being so impetuous. I long for you in the day, and I… I didn't mean to… Psyche, I want you to have pleasure, too." He took her hand and kissed it tenderly. Then he put it on her mound.

"Touch yourself. Here." Covering her fingers with his own, he pushed them into her sex.

She did as he said, feeling herself for the first time. She was not sticky with desire, but wet from his fluid. She rubbed herself lightly, his hand guiding her. He kissed her ear, his hot breath making her shiver as his fingers danced above her own. She delved into her sex and found the nub that brought her such pleasure. He pushed her finger deeper and she discovered how wet and warm she was. She began to understand why he wanted to be inside her.

He moved his mouth from her ear to her throat, biting her gently. His lips moved back to her breast, still ravenous for her. As he devoured her nipples, she thought of a snake, eating her whole. She would not resist anything he did to her. She had given him her heart.

As her fingers stroked her nub, she began to rouse herself. He hardened against her hip, ready to take her again as she arched her back, opening herself to him more, giving him her breasts to feed on.

"Yes," he said, "like that, Psyche."

Glad no lamps were lit, she continued to touch herself, burning with shame and desire.

He moved atop her, sliding the head of his shaft into her, but staying still.

"Make yourself come into your pleasure, Psyche."

Despite the dark, she wanted to cover her face, but his hand trapped her left wrist against her side. She did as he said and, opening her legs, stroked herself until she shuddered against him, her sex spasming against the tip of his shaft, which he plunged deep inside her.

He began to move in her in earnest, making her quiver with desire. He again took her nipple into his mouth and sucked hard. *Devour me*, she thought, *take me completely.* She did not think it could happen again, but as he thrust harder and harder against her, her pleasure mounted, bringing her to the brink.

"Please," she begged, not even knowing she was speaking.

She heard him laugh as he pounded against her with his full force. Her climax was instant. Her body both yielded and tightened against him, squeezing the seed from his shaft so hard she saw stars behind her eyes. And then, floating in the blue sky, she saw the golden eyes of the winged one.

She opened her own eyes but saw only darkness. Her husband moved off her.

"I hope I made up for my early lapse," he said, amusement in his voice.

"Yes. I did not realize I could… that you could." Her breathing was just beginning to slow. It had been as if her whole body was an earthquake. He put the palm of his hand on her mound and she trembled with an aftershock of desire.

"No," she said panting, "please." But he ignored her protests, and with the slightest movement of his finger, made her hips rise. He laughed and bit her ear, making her come into her pleasure again and again.

She should have slept all night. But the sugar in the wine and her conflicting thoughts woke her. He must be a god, she thought excitedly. He had all but told her himself. She had truly loved him all along. He was the winged one!

The wine whispered to her again. *But, no, what were monsters but the children of gods and Titans? They too could spawn divine children. He could be the Day Killer, a monstrous snake.* Terror gripped her, as it can only in the dark of night. She loved him, but he had been so rough with her tonight. Though she had enjoyed what had happened after, she could not help but wonder if this marked the beginning of his change. If once she bore his child, would he be done with her? *Or, perhaps he would eat the child straight from her womb.*

Rolling away from him, she realized her fate had been decided, and neither her husband nor her own heart could prevent her from breaking a second promise.

Just a peek. The wine still sang as she slipped out of bed. She did not want to betray him, but there was no other way to know who he was. His child grew in her belly, yet in the midst of her deepest pleasure, she imagined the winged one. Was he her husband or was she being disloyal by wishing he was someone else?

She went down the stairs and into the kitchen for the lamp and the knife. Her heart pounded in fear, but there was no turning back. She must know. If he was the winged one, she could live with him in the darkness forever. If he was some hideous creature, she would love him anyway. And if she could not, she would kill herself.

The shadows danced as she reentered their bedroom. She forced her hand to hold still as she approached the bed and parted the curtain. The light caught the silhouette of his shoulder golden from the sun, not green like a snake. She could have stopped then. Just seeing his flesh could have been enough. But no, she had to see his face.

She held the lamp up. The light revealed that his hair was dark and wild. The shadows played on his cheeks, his lips, his lashes. He was beautiful. She moved the lamp lower, to gaze at his sleek wings, soft and brown as she remembered, the same color of his wild hair.

He was divine. She had not betrayed him in her heart but had loved him more. She had not been unfaithful. Her shadow husband was the one of her dreams. He was the winged one. She had been chosen by the God of Love!

But the lamp also seemed to rejoice, and wanting to touch him, a drop of oil fell onto his shoulder. She watched the tiny bead of hot oil in horror, knowing she could not stop it.

He awoke with a cry of surprise. His golden eyes opened in pain, and he rose from the bed, not as a mortal but as a god. His wings flew open, splitting the bed curtains. She backed away, wishing the darkness could hide her, but the lamp she held made it impossible to deny her crime. His face filled with fury.

"Wicked woman, you have betrayed me!" His voice was not the one she knew, but that of the monsters she had imagined. He came at her, towering above her, his wings spread wide. "I did not want to hurt you, Psyche, but now you will know why gods and men fear me. Now you will know my wrath!"

"Please, husband." She knelt before him, her heart breaking. Her hands shook and she set down the lamp.

"What is this?" he asked, spying the knife in her other hand. "Is this how you repay love? I went against my mother for you. And you, faithless mortal, you would try to kill me?"

"No, husband, I would never hurt you. This knife is for me. If you leave me, I will die. Please do not forsake me."

His eyes met hers and for a moment she was back in his arms the first time he had carried her over the sea. He stepped closer, his eyes brimming with silver tears.

"But you have hurt me more than anyone. And your punishment will match my pain." He grabbed the knife from her hands and threw it across the room. "I forbid you from taking your life, Psyche. You must live with the misery you have caused us both. I did not want to leave you. I wanted to see our child born, for her to be divine, but now you must suffer alone. Another wretched woman, unworthy of love."

He turned to leave. Unwilling to let love go so easily, she followed him to the balcony.

"No," she said again. "Please."

"Love cannot live without trust," he said, spreading his wings to fly away. She ran to him and grasped his waist as he took flight. Her unexpected weight upset the balance and he struggled to be airborne for a moment before righting himself. She hoped he would either pull her up into his arms or fling her to the earth so she could die. But he did neither, flying low to the ground instead.

She held him tightly as he flew. Her arms clenched around his waist, her mouth on his hipbone, kissing him there, knowing he would push her away, that she had been given the gift of love and in her curiosity had lost all. The pain would come soon, but she savored her lips on his flesh if only for one more moment.

"Let go, Psyche. Don't make me hurt you more than I have to."

"I would suffer any pain if it meant not losing you. Please, husband, beat me, punish me yourself, but do not abandon me."

"Oh, wretched woman," he said, stroking her face. "You knew it was forbidden to look on me. You broke your promise. Now you will know the sting of my arrow. I will do as you ask and punish you myself, but not as your earthly husband. Now you will learn how the God of Love punishes all. When I am done with you, Psyche, you will see that I truly am a monster." He pried her hands from his hips and dropped her.

She expected to fall hard, to break something, to die, but he had flown low and dropped her above a grassy field.

"No!" she cried, struggling to regain her breath. "No," she cried, her voice too small for him to hear as he flew higher and higher. "Love forgives," she said, as tears coursed down her cheeks. "Love can be renewed," she whispered. "Love returns!" She lay where he had left her, weeping bitter tears until the sun rose.

PART TWO

THE TRIALS OF PSYCHE

Shrouded by sorrow, Psyche wandered aimlessly. But in cruelty or compassion, her husband had left her near the kingdom of her sister Iris; and before midday hunters found her. Hoping for a reward, they brought her to their queen.

Iris did not try to hide her delight in seeing Psyche reduced to such a pitiful state.

"Little sister, what has befallen you? I can barely recognize you with your golden hair tangled like a madwoman's. Your beauty is still intact, Psyche, but it is dull like an unpolished gem. Was it only yesterday that you were so radiant and beautiful—as if you were truly the second coming of Venus?"

The fullness of her loss overtook her and Psyche could make no response other than a small sound like that of a wounded animal.

Iris stepped next to her sister and opened the shawl she had been wrapped in by the huntsmen.

"Oh, little sister, did your husband turn you out naked? It does not look like he beat you, though"—Iris inhaled through her nose —"it smells as if he had you before pushing you out of his house. You smell like sex, little sister, and dirt. Did you sleep in the mud?

If I didn't know you, Psyche, I would never guess you were a princess, only a pretty beggar. Come, let's take you to the baths, though with all that dirt, perhaps the slaves' baths would be best—we want to avoid a scandal, don't we?"

Even through the cloud of her depression, Psyche knew that the slaves would gossip more than anyone. But it did not matter what other mortals said or thought of her. Psyche cared only for the opinion of one being, and he did not live in her sister's palace.

After being bathed, fed, and dressed in a rather plain sky blue gown, Iris summoned her sister to her chamber. Psyche immediately noticed a golden statue Iris had taken from her house of Jupiter seducing Leda in the shape of a swan. The long neck wrapped around Leda's body, as if there were no possibility of escape. All the statues in the monster's palace had been of gods seducing mortals—why had she not just been content with that?

"What happened, darling girl?" Iris asked, offering Psyche a plain clay cup filled with wine. Psyche raised the cup to her lips as her sister filled her own golden one. Gold and jewels did not matter to Psyche now. She wished to tell Iris this, but there was no point. Iris would never understand the bond Psyche had with her husband. It was better to just give her what she wanted to hear.

"Sister, my husband is none other than the God of Love. I heeded your words and betrayed him. The oil from the lamp burned him. He awoke in a fury and cast me out." Tears overwhelmed her and for a moment she could not speak. The delight in her sister's blue eyes lit a spark of anger in Psyche. Before she even knew what she was saying, lies rushed from her throat.

"But he saw you, sister, and when he left me, he said he would take you in my stead."

Iris's eyes grew wide with glee and she licked her lips. With a will of their own, her hands went to her hair to smooth it out. The part was perfect. She was as well kempt as Psyche was disheveled.

Simply imagining that the lie was real was like a knife to Psyche's throat. Tears overflowed her eyes, and pain came at her in waves as she sensed how much Iris enjoyed this fantasy.

"But, sister, elder, I know you would never betray me that way," Psyche continued. "You cannot imagine how my heart breaks. Though I believe I deserve my punishment for disobeying my husband, it would be too much to bear for you to take my place. Besides, I know you love your husband, your kingdom, and your children."

"Yes, of course. How this loss must pain you, little sister. What else did he say?"

"Only that if you agree to be his, to go to where Lord Zephyr left you. But I told him you would not do it."

"Of course not. Poor Psyche, such a blow to lose a god. And the God of Love, so handsome and strong... I can't believe he wants me..." Iris grinned.

Indeed, her eldest sister was beautiful on the outside. Jealousy overtook Psyche, imagining her husband with Iris. But he would see her for the viper she truly was.

"I am flattered," Iris said, smoothing out her hair again, "but I would never... Just rest, little Psyche, stay here as long as you like... I need to attend to..." Iris did not bother to complete the lie. She just walked quickly away.

Even locked in her sorrow, Psyche almost laughed to see her sister struggle to keep the joy from her face, not to run out of the palace. But after Iris left, regret gripped Psyche. She was neither cruel nor a liar. At least she had not been these things before. Now she saw how the barbs of love worked. Having been pierced, she wanted to cause pain to one who had hurt her.

The next day Iris was missing. Psyche tried to push her guilt away, telling herself her sister had made her own choice. Taking only a basket of food and a cloak, Psyche left in the confusion before her sister's broken body was found at the bottom of the mountain.

DRESSED IN A SKY BLUE *STOLA*, and a dark blue shawl, Psyche began to wander. She had no clear destination, but she needed to keep moving, as if she could somehow escape her heartbreak.

Despite how dangerous it was for a woman to travel alone, no great evil befell her. At first she expected to be taken by men, raped or enslaved, though in her grief she did not care for her own safety. Her husband had forbidden her from taking her own life, but she could tempt fate and find another to kill her.

Yet, no bandits jumped out from behind trees, no thieves or slavers accosted her. Instead, more than once, she found herself coming upon a farm near sunset where a kindly wife would invite her in, giving her stew and bread and a warm place to sleep. Or, if she was far from people and she decided to just lie down in the woods, careless to her own comfort, almost hoping that wolves would come eat her, she would instead discover a soft place to sleep, a bed of grass amongst fallen pine needles, or a shepherd or woodcutter would come along and invite her to come to his humble house, to eat the dinner his wife had prepared, to share a bed with his daughter. Psyche had no proof her husband did these things for her, but each time a stranger was kind to her, and each time a man did not ask her to marry him, it gave her hope that the God of Love watched over her.

Along the way she stopped to pray at each temple she came to. Having no sacrifice, she did what she could to clean or help the priestesses or novices. She was surprised to find many temples empty. The gods were being neglected. Faith was changing.

She found Ceres's temple deserted. A mess of grain was scattered on the ground, the altar stone empty. After cleaning as best she could, Psyche found some oil and lit a lamp. Outside there were fig trees and she picked the ripe ones to leave for the goddess. As she did at every temple, she prayed for Venus's mercy. Only this time, when her prayer was done, the Goddess of the Grain appeared.

Ceres's hair was the color of wheat and her eyes the color of fertile soil. Her brown and green gown was woven from wool, flowers, and leaves, and smelled of earth and the most fragrant blossoms.

"You must be Psyche," the goddess said. "Oh, but you are a beauty, even in your misery. I can imagine how lovely you are in full bloom! I can see why Venus would hate you. Hmm." Ceres placed her hand on Psyche's cheek and the goddess's energy warmed her. She inserted her hand inside Psyche's *stola*, just above her breast, placing her palm flat over her heart. Psyche felt as if she was a flower being warmed by the sun, dry soil watered by sweet rain. Ceres looked deep into her eyes.

"You feel me," Ceres said. "You feel the divine in a way most mortals do not." She pulled her hand away and studied Psyche's face.

"Are you your father's daughter? Did your mother ever tell you of a dream she had before conceiving you? I'm wondering if you are not a child of Zeus, or perhaps Hermes, that rascal, always getting about."

"No," Psyche said. "I am my father's child. I have his eyes— they are the same shade of blue. And his ears and nose, though mine are smaller."

"Hmm," Ceres said. "Well, perhaps one of your grandparents was a demigod, sometimes it skips a generation, but I do not think you're only a mortal—such beauty and such… awareness." She caressed Psyche's cheek. "And I can feel your pain. For I alone among the gods remember what it is to have your heart broken." She moved her hand to Psyche's belly. "And there is a life in here. A small seed has taken root and it grows. You must take better care of yourself, child. You have my permission to eat any of the food that grows from my earth." She opened her hand and gave Psyche bread and apples. Psyche suddenly felt the hunger she had denied herself and ate what the goddess gave her.

"I cannot intervene on your behalf, Psyche. I try to keep the peace among the gods. Though I've heard that Venus looks for you. Go to her and beg mercy. Your beloved is in her heavenly palace nursing his wounds. Though I know little about the love between the sexes, I dare say his heart is hurt more than his shoulder. It seems that in punishing you, he has punished himself."

At the mention of her husband, Psyche felt a stirring of hope, but when she thought of his mother, she grew cold with fear. Venus had hated her before, and now Psyche had injured her son. But if there was any chance of seeing him again, even if she risked death, she would do it gladly.

Ceres stroked Psyche's cheek one last time. "I must go, for my daughter's time to return to her husband draws near, and I want to be with her before my heart is ripped out again. I know your pain, child, and I hope you find peace."

And with that Ceres disappeared, leaving Psyche with such a sense of melancholy that she knelt on the ground and wept.

CHAPTER 6

VENUS'S TEMPLE

Psyche heeded Ceres's advice and wandered until she found her way to a temple of Venus. The pathway was untended and the cobwebs showed that no one had come for some time. Even the priestesses seemed to have abandoned the place. Psyche found some oil and lit a lamp.

"Goddess of Love and Beauty, please hear me and come aid my miserable heart. I have come to beg your forgiveness." She knelt at the altar listening to the wind. "Goddess, it is Psyche. I fear you seek me and if you do, I await you here as your servant."

Animosity filled the temple, as heavy as a woolen cloak suddenly upon her shoulders, though nothing appeared to have changed.

"Strip off your clothes, mortal," the goddess's voice said. "You will hide nothing from me now."

Psyche struggled to remove her *stola*. She was used to having a slave help with her clothes; even during her wandering it seemed a farmer's wife or temple slave was always available to assist her. Finally, she managed to remove the *stola*, and the tunic she wore underneath.

When she was naked, Venus appeared. The goddess loomed

62

above Psyche wearing a shimmering red gown, embroidered with silver and gold thread, glittering with rubies. Venus's eyes were black and seemed to be filled with delight and anger.

"Still beautiful," Venus said, her fingers brushing Psyche's chest. The goddess's touch brought buzzing pleasure, even stronger than the first time. It was as if the goddess was reaching into her body, probing her emotions. "Even in your misery, you are still more beautiful than any other mortal."

"No," Psyche whispered. "How could that possibly be true? If I were, he would not have left me."

"But you are still just a mortal," Venus said. "Where's your sacrifice?"

"I am the sacrifice, goddess. Though I am no longer a virgin, I believe you might want me still. Though I beg you, goddess, before I die, will you permit me to see my husband one last time? There is something I must tell him."

"Husband," the goddess said, the word poison in her mouth. "My son is not your husband. You were just his plaything, and he is done playing with you now." She took Psyche by the throat and lifted her. Psyche grasped at the goddess's wrist and kicked her legs. She had sought out the goddess to find her love or die, and it seemed Venus was happy to fulfill her dark wish. Even as she struggled to breathe, the goddess's touch radiated pleasure.

"Tell him," Psyche whispered, "that I died begging his forgiveness, that I will always love him."

Something flickered in Venus's eyes and Psyche felt the emptiness in the goddess's heart.

"Mars," Psyche whispered with her last bit of air. "Lord Mars, come."

He was not usually so easily summoned. However, it was a time of peace, and there were not enough sacrifices to the God of War. But perhaps even in times of war, the dying plea of the most beautiful girl, dangling naked in Venus's temple would have enticed him.

Through the darkness that had begun to cloud Psyche's eyes, she saw him appear in a flash of light and smoke, revealing only armor, muscle, and heat.

"Queen of Beauty," he said, "it is my work to murder mortals. If you kill her, must I make a warrior so beautiful that all his comrades fall in love with him? A warrior so stunning that the war ceases and dissolves into an orgy?"

Venus laughed at the thought and released the girl. Psyche crumbled onto the cold floor, gasping, grateful for the cool marble on her cheek. After recovering her breath, she gazed up at Mars. Tall, with long black hair and bulging muscles, he was the pinnacle of male strength. His black helm and black leather tunic smelled of smoke, leather, and blood.

Psyche lay on the ground staring at the defined muscles of his calves and thighs, but when she looked past his broad chest and into his face, she was filled with terror. Though he was classically handsome, with a fine Roman nose and black flowing beard, the power of the lives he had taken and the desire to take more emanated from him. The force of his power was so overwhelming she thought she might be ill.

As soon as Venus had dropped her, the two gods forgot about her. Sparks flew between their eyes.

"Why has it been so long since I've seen you?" Mars asked.

"You angered me. I cannot remember what you did, only that I was filled with hate."

"Yes," Mars said, "I have that effect. But you, beloved, most beautiful in all the world, you fill me only with love and longing." He strode toward her and stroked her white neck with his large hands. Psyche tried to avert her gaze. Gazing upon Venus filled her with desire, but seeing Mars brought the fear back. Yet she could not take her eyes off either of them.

"I long for you, beloved," Mars said. "I yearn to behold your beauty, to revel in your perfection. Lovely goddess, I need to caress your conch, to tongue your pearl." Mars tried to take Venus's hand, but she pushed him away.

"Leave poetry for the poets, brother. There's only one thing your mouth is good for."

Venus grinned wickedly and slowly lifted her red gown. Her thighs were the color of alabaster. Psyche would never again have that pure color, forever marked by the hand of the winged one. The goddess lifted her dress higher and flashed her vulva at Mars. Fear of being remembered kept Psyche from gasping aloud. The hair there was the color of pure gold.

Venus lowered her gown and Mars knelt at her feet. She lifted one strong leg and rested her sandaled foot on his shoulder. His eyes pooled with desire and he kissed her ankle and her calf, holding her thigh in his muscular arms. He crept closer to her on his knees, her foot trailing over his shoulder to his back. Venus smiled as the god kissed her creamy skin, licked the flesh of her thigh, and lifted her gown to see the jewel beneath.

A golden throne appeared behind Venus and with a contented sigh, she sat back while Mars stayed on his knees urgent to please her. The Goddess of Love and Beauty spread her legs wide and, gripping the God of War by the hair, pulled his face into her.

Mars moaned with desire and his sounds of pleasure were soon mingled with the goddess's. Psyche could not avert her eyes from the way his thick, full head of black hair thrust back and forth between the goddess's legs, like a hungry lion gorging himself on a freshly killed gazelle.

With one elegant hand, Venus opened her gown and brought out her perfect breast, pearly white with a nipple the color of the rosy dawn. The goddess caressed herself, pinching her nipple as Mars grunted and licked her below. Watching them flooded Psyche with desire. She had never imagined a woman could have so much control over her pleasure.

Venus's eyes grew heavy lidded as she gripped Mars's hair with her fist, thrusting her sex into his mouth. He pulled back and licked her tenderly, until Psyche could hear the need in her moans.

Mars suddenly pulled away. "Beloved," he said, his eyes aflame, "take me."

There was a silent war between the gods then. It seemed Venus did not want to give herself to him in the usual way. She wanted him only on his knees. Mars stroked her inner thigh with his war-hardened hands and taunted her with pleasure. In the end, she gave in.

A golden couch rose from the marble floor of the temple.

"Go on," Venus said, her throaty voice cold but full of desire.

Mars lay on the couch, the way a woman would await her husband in the marriage bed. The goddess climbed atop him. With one touch of her hand, his clothing disappeared though she was still dressed. He sighed as she stripped him through pure will. As his eyes rolled back, he caught sight of Psyche on the floor.

"The mortal. Should I kill her for you?"

"No," the goddess said, a wicked smile lifting her lips. "Let her watch. We can kill her after."

Mars looked greedily at the girl; both ideas aroused him.

Completely mesmerized by the spectacle she was sure would be her last, Psyche no longer tried to look away.

Mars caressed Venus's breast, taking her nipple between his forefinger and thumb, as if plucking a grape and slowly drew it into his mouth.

There was a deep throb low in Psyche's belly. Her fear when first looking upon him had changed to desire, and she felt the pure passion of men about to kill. She had never thought of the power of men at war but now, watching the god, all she wanted to do was to thrust her sword into the submissive body of an enemy over and over again.

The temple shook as Venus straddled Mars and lowered herself onto him. After the time with his tongue, her pleasure was instant. She arched her back and moaned. Psyche was fascinated to see the goddess's eyes close in ecstasy, as if for one moment, she had finally found peace. Venus stayed still, shuddering on top of Mars, who watched her with a delighted grin on his lips.

Soon Venus seemed to recover and Psyche was hypnotized by the way their bodies undulated like waves in the sea, like a snake moving quickly after its prey. Venus rode him hard and fast and then, with that wicked grin upon her lips, moved slowly, ever so slowly.

"I am not done with you, brother. Stay hard for me," she said, gripping his nipples. The God of War moaned as she trapped him between her thighs, forcing him to cry out for her. And the Goddess of Love, on top, took her time with her pleasure until Mars clenched his jaw, struggling to keep himself for her.

If they had not already decided to kill her, this, seeing this would have been enough. Then the goddess turned her eyes on Psyche and the girl was flooded with the goddess's power, and with her pleasure. Psyche writhed on the cold mosaic as if she were the one taking the God of War. She did not understand what was happening, but as the goddess came into her pleasure a second time, Psyche came with her, crying out in unison. Mars finally allowed himself to relax and released his seed in a frothy wave, cleaving to the goddess until he spent himself deep inside her.

Glistening with golden sweat, the gods reclined on their couch, eyes closed, slowly disentangling themselves. Psyche wondered if they would sleep and if they did, if she should try to escape. But Mars roused himself. Rolling onto his side, he leaned on an elbow, propped his head in his hand, and gazed at his goddess.

"You are the only one who can do that to me."

"Yet I am not the only one you have," Venus said, danger in her voice.

"Beloved, you are married." Then seeing the steel in her eyes, he kissed her shoulder. "You are the only one I love. I would do anything for you."

"Kill that girl."

"Of course," he said, lifting his hand.

"Please, Lord Mars," Psyche said, suddenly feeling the urge to fight, "I beg you, tell your son I await him in Hades. Tell him I will always love him. Please."

Mars pulled his hand back. "What now?" He turned to the goddess. "Who is this girl?"

"No one. Just some mortal. Well born, beautiful, but nothing to us."

"Forgive me, goddess. I am your son's wife. His child grows in my womb." She dared rise no higher than her knees, but she did rise.

"Kill her, brother."

"Please ask your son if he wants me that way. If he does, I would go gladly to my death. He has forbidden me from taking my own life, or else I would have, for I have died a thousand times without him."

The fury in the goddess's eyes blazed, but Mars stared at Psyche oddly.

"Does our son love this woman, this mortal?"

"Yes," Venus admitted.

"Did he prick himself with his arrow?"

"Yes. But it was more than that. This girl has some kind of magic of her own. She has been nothing but trouble to me."

"Please," Psyche said, the feeling of war making her bold, "goddess, forgive me, but I feel I understand you. I don't want to take anything that is yours, but I feel that I know your will as if it were my own."

The goddess was upon her before she could finish. She slapped Psyche and knocked her to the ground, but Mars stopped Venus from striking her again.

"Beloved, do you not see what she means? In these times when mortals are so fickle, this girl offers you devotion. How many times have you passed a gathering, a wedding even, without the slightest reaction? This girl feels us. This girl worships us. There is nothing divine about her, but she is of the gods." Venus lifted her hand to strike him, but he caught her wrist.

"My love, Queen of Beauty, why should this girl threaten you? Look at her! She has a pretty face, but nothing like yours. Her hair is golden, but yours is gold." He regarded Psyche with curiosity. "Stand up, mortal."

She did as he said, trembling, but forcing herself to look into his eyes. The terror she saw there made her look away quickly, for she could see the thousands, the millions of lives he had taken, and that his desire to kill would never be sated.

His hand was suddenly on her tender breast, squeezing until she yelped.

"Her breasts might be pert, but they are too big. Her figure is shapely, her belly is slightly rounded as a woman's should be. But her hips"—he put his rough hands on them as she quivered—"too narrow. She is barely a woman, my love. Her beauty pales in comparison to yours. And her skin, what is this? She looks like a farmer's wife with these marks."

Enjoying Mars's comparison, Venus returned to her couch. Her laughter rang like bells as each of Psyche's defects was listed. But Venus did not see the true hunger in the God of War's eyes. Psyche did not know which she feared more, the God of War's desire for her or Venus seeing it.

"Turn around," he commanded, curious to solve the mystery of her discoloration.

She turned and let him see her backside. His laugh was like a dog barking.

"Look at this, beloved. Did you see this? Bend over, girl."

All the blood rushed to Psyche's face. She had no choice but to bend at the waist, so her golden hair fell to the floor of the temple, giving the gods a full view of her crevice.

The God of War stroked the buttock the winged one had marked, blocking her body from Venus's view with his own. He slid one rough finger from her moist bud, to her sopping chasm, all the way to her rear. She bit her lip not to gasp. If Venus saw, she would kill her twice.

Mars touched the spot the winged one had marked, where Psyche knew there was a white imprint from his hand. Mars hissed suddenly, pulling away.

"Ouch," he said evenly, though she heard a whisper in his voice that might mask pain. She was surprised that he would be in any way sympathetic.

"Look at this," he said, stepping aside for the goddess to see. "He has marked her and claimed her as his own."

Done with Psyche, he returned to Venus on the couch.

He had not given Psyche permission to stand, but she would not remain in that humiliating position a moment longer. She bent her knees and knelt on the ground, slowly turning around.

The air in the temple felt suddenly heavy with the goddess's anger not just at Psyche, but at Mars who could receive it better.

Had the goddess seen him touch her? The gods were back on their golden couch struggling, Venus trying to hit him; Mars preventing her from it.

"All right," he said suddenly. "I will not come between the war of women. Kill her if you wish, beloved, but ask yourself if our son will forgive you for it. He is becoming a man. Has he ever marked a mortal as his own before? Has he ever bedded a mortal, or a nymph for that matter? We know he is fickle and foolish, but this girl does not seem such a bad daughter-in-law. She should be no threat to you, beloved, for you are above all creatures. And she is just a girl, not even half as beautiful as you.

"But I would never presume to tell you what to do. Let me see our son. Tell me where he is and I will leave you to fulfill your will."

Venus spoke coldly to the God of War. "He is in my palace, recovering from the wounds this creature gave him. Go to him. Get him to agree to let me kill her."

Mars took Venus's hand, kissed it and disappeared. The goddess turned her gaze on Psyche.

"You are smarter than you look, little beast. How clever of you to summon the God of War. I won't kill you today, but you have further roused my anger, and I will punish you for it." The goddess's eyes lit up as she contemplated how to torment the girl. Then she smiled, and dread gripped Psyche's belly like a claw.

CHAPTER 7

CARE AND SORROW

Trembling with cold and fear, Psyche knelt where Mars had left her. She kept her eyes lowered, the mosaics on the floor of lovers cavorting mocked her. Venus rose from her couch and stared down at her. The goddess stroked her own golden hair in contemplation.

"What shall I do with you?" Venus asked, coming closer. "What would the best punishment be for the little vixen who my son betrayed me for, who dared called the God of War to save her life? How should I torment the girl whose beauty took worshippers out of my temple?"

As Venus circled her, the red silk of her dress gently brushed Psyche's thigh. The goddess smelled of roses and sex. Traces of the scent of the God of War of smoke and leather still lingered.

Even as Venus glared down in contempt, Psyche was struck by the goddess's beauty. She wished desperately that those eyes would look on her in mercy. An idea seemed to have come to the goddess and her grin widened, showing her perfectly white teeth.

"It was good you dissuaded Mars from killing you, little beast. Now I have a chance to play with you as a cat plays with a mouse before dismembering it."

Psyche swallowed, hoping the goddess would be like some of the palace cats who lost interest in the mouse before killing it.

"Please, goddess, I never meant to anger you. I am your most devoted servant."

Venus laughed, a light clear sound, like bells ringing. She turned away and went to her golden throne where she reclined, her eyes twinkling in amusement at the girl's terror.

"My servant... yes. Come over here then and come on your knees."

The space between them was not great, but Psyche moved slowly over the mosaics, the little pieces of stone and tile digging into her knees and shins until she got to the smooth white marble before Venus's throne. Venus leaned forward and grasped Psyche's chin, raising the girl's face so Psyche had no choice but to look the goddess in the eyes.

"You are more like an errant slave, deserving a peerless punishment. Yet perhaps I should allow you the great honor of serving in one of my temples? After all, you were thought to be the 'second coming of Venus.' Why not give the people what they want?"

Venus stroked Psyche's golden tresses. Her once carefully coiffed hair had come unbound. Psyche could not remember the last time she had brushed it. Despite her circumstances, it was unseemly to appear before the Goddess of Love and Beauty with her golden locks curling naturally and falling wild like a barbarian. Venus gathered it all into her hands and then dropped her hair so if fell over Psyche's shoulders.

"When you serve as my priestess, this will be your only garment."

Venus placed her thumb and middle finger on Psyche's temples. The goddess's touch was cool and hard as if made of marble, but still any contact Psyche had with the goddess brought vibrations of pleasure, even while the images the goddess sent flashed through her mind.

In Venus's vision, the empty unkempt temple they were in was completely changed. No longer covered with dust, the marble sparkled white. The building was full of noise, offerings and devotees. Transparent pink silk curtains fluttered, giving the illusion of privacy. Psyche saw her own face, her eyes squeezed tight, as if to block out the light. Venus stroked Psyche's temple showing her the full picture—Psyche naked, lying under a hairy man who panted and grunted atop her. Behind the pink curtains was a never-ending line of men waiting for her to please them. The men were old and young, rich and poor, handsome and ugly. Some were ill and malformed, but as a temple priestess, Psyche could deny none. A wave of nausea hit her as the goddess pushed more images into her mind. An old, bald, one-legged veteran, nearly toothless, came to her couch, ready to worship the goddess. Psyche in Venus's mind—pale, haggard, ensconced in misery—needed to accommodate the veteran by sitting atop him. Psyche tried to pull away, but Venus held her fast, forcing her to watch herself ride the man as he pawed at her breasts with his sausage like fingers.

"Yes," Venus said. "A king's daughter, the most famous sacred whore in all the land. It will bring all the worshipers back to me. This is what I should have done with you to begin with…" Venus paused, her eyes narrowing. "I would have done it sooner, but when all this business with you started, my son said he would take care of you…" The goddess's eyes changed from blue to black. "He was supposed to shoot you and make you love a beggar. You were to be a laughingstock. But when he saw you, he pricked himself on accident and could not tolerate the thought of anyone else having you."

Psyche gasped and pulled away, remembering the first time she had felt his presence. After her bath, the first time she had spoken aloud to herself. It had been him all along! She struggled to recall the other times she had felt the hair on the back of her neck rise, but Venus gripped her jaw.

"Three years passed, little beast, and still the people did not return to my temples, talking instead of your beauty. My son kept making excuses for not shooting you. I never would have guessed that he wanted you for himself! And then he and Apollo, and probably that scoundrel Hermes, tricked me with a false prophecy that you were to be given to a monster. And to make up for all the times he had disappointed me, my son promised to take you to the monster himself. He said he would shoot you with a golden arrow, so you loved the monster, but he would shoot the monster with lead, so he would disdain you." Venus laughed at the thought. "And I was happy knowing of your misery, but he lied to me!" She squeezed Psyche's jaw and stroked the bruises on her throat.

"So, thank you, little beast, for saving your own life. Death is too much of a gift for you. Now you will serve men in my temple."

"Goddess, does my husband know I am here? Does he… want this of me?"

Venus laughed. "I'm sure he won't want you after your service is complete. Come, my most devoted servant, I shall initiate you as a priestess." Venus grasped Psyche's wrist and began to pull her up, but the girl stayed on her knees.

"If my husband commands it, I will"—she forced herself to say the words—"serve in your temple. But only if he himself tells me to do it."

Venus's grasp became rough on Psyche's wrist, squeezing and pinching until Psyche yelped. Yet even through the pain, Psyche could feel the buzzing vibration of pleasure.

"Please, goddess," she cried.

Venus released her, a new idea seeming to come into her mind.

"I like hearing you beg. I will call my handmaidens, Sorrow and Care, and they will make you beg some more." Venus clapped her hands, and two lesser goddesses appeared.

Sorrow, gray-skinned with hair black as night, had the face of a young girl made old by grief. Dark rivers of wrinkles covered her sallow face, each another heartbreak. Her body was thin, like a bitter crone. But there was steel in her spine, ready to endure more torment. Her eyes may have once been gray, but the whites of her eyes, reddened from so many tears, made her irises shine white in contrast. She wore a dove-gray gown, threaded with black pearls reminiscent of tears. Her girdle was black iron with black silk cords wrapped tightly around her narrow waist.

Care was a stout goddess with big hands. Her eyes burned bright orange, searching for things that could never be found, worrying for all that could be, as well as for all that could not. Her hair was white-blond but thin, for she pulled at it constantly. Her hands could not rest, nor could her body. She twitched nervously. Multicolored fabrics of various woes had been stitched together to make a gown fragmented with a rainbow of worries. Different colored ribbons were wrapped around her waist. Psyche noticed how Care fingered a thick red silk sash, worrying it with her fingers; the nails were bitten to the quick.

"Goddess," Care said, her voice was high-pitched, like a mouse squeaking in fear, "how may we serve you?"

"This girl, my least faithful servant, has provoked my anger."

Sorrow and Care surrounded Psyche. For a moment, Sorrow looked happy and Care's eyes brightened at an easy task. Like Venus, they towered over the trembling mortal. They each took one of Psyche's arms and pulled her up. Their hands upon her, like cruel steel, flooded Psyche with their pain. She shuddered at their touch, but knew there would be no escape.

"How shall we punish her, goddess?" Sorrow asked, her voice like pebbles being kicked.

Venus eyed her rival, savoring her fear. "I haven't decided yet. Hold her higher."

Grabbing her wrists, Care pulled Psyche to her tiptoes, holding the girl's wrists in a vice grip above her head.

"So many places we can torment," the goddess said. "Bring her closer." Venus stretched out her beautiful white hand and touched the bruises on Psyche's throat, slowly trailing her hand to Psyche's breast. When Venus took Psyche's nipple between her thumb and forefinger, pleasure flooded her even as the goddess squeezed cruelly. She gasped and struggled against the manacle of Care's hands, hating herself for wishing the goddess would touch her again.

"Such a soft thing, these creatures of flesh and blood," Venus said to Sorrow who stood watching. Venus ran her hand down Psyche's breast to her pubis, barely touching the hair there, yet her whole body buzzed with sensation and she stifled a moan.

Venus laughed at the girl's desire. "And this one is especially sensitive. Turn her."

As if holding a doll, Care rotated Psyche so her back was to the goddess. Was the God of Love's mark still there? Psyche dared not turn her head to check. Venus stood and gathered Psyche's wild hair in her hands as she had the first time they met. She pulled at a snarl and ran her nails over the back of Psyche's neck, scratching her softly.

"I'm sure you wish you could grow wings," the goddess said, stroking Psyche's shoulder blades. Her light touch sent images into the girl's mind. Psyche saw herself as the goddess saw her, from behind, held taut with her arms above her head. But now Venus envisioned her with blue butterfly wings. They were so real that she could feel them, silken, gossamer, so light and yet strong enough to let her fly away.

Tears flooded Psyche's eyes with the realization that she had always wanted to have wings of her own. And the ones the goddess had given her were exceptionally beautiful—iridescent blue, ready to flutter in the sunlight. Black lines decorated her wings with two white circles, eyes to frighten predators. Summoning a muscle she had not known she possessed, Psyche began to move her wings. Slowly they began to flutter. Ever so gently, they brushed her skin. She pushed harder and the wings began to beat up and down. Of course the goddess would never let her escape, but just the sensation of having wings, of creating her own wind, was pure pleasure. Beating them harder, she was suddenly lifted off the ground. Care still gripped her wrists, but for a moment Psyche felt she could take flight. Like her husband, she could fly!

"Ah," Venus said, "now you are beautiful. Now you are special." She stroked the back of Psyche's neck and ran her hand down the girl's spine between her wings. "You have always wanted to fly away, haven't you, little beast? To fly above all the pettiness of your kind, the poor politics of your kingdom."

She patted Psyche's right buttock with approval. "Yes, now you could be my devoted servant. If you take this gift, I will fill you with love and beauty." Venus touched the delicate spot where the wings met Psyche's flesh, filling her with radiance and warmth, a feeling of complete satisfaction. But even ensconced in the glow of the goddess's touch, Psyche felt an emptiness that only her beloved could fill.

"If I were to give you these, would you stop troubling yourself with my son?"

Psyche hovered just a little off the ground, half turning though still held by Care. She had never seen the goddess look at her this way. There was no compassion in the goddess's eyes, but neither was there hate. Psyche realized it was curiosity, as if for the first time the goddess had been intrigued by a mortal woman.

"What would you do, little beast, if I were to let you go right now?"

Psyche imagined herself released by Care, all her worries staying behind as she flew out of the goddess's temple, away from the anger of Venus. To have her own freedom, to fly naked through the sky with her hair unbound, as if she too were a god! She tried to foresee her new life, living alone, away from mortals and gods, or making new friends and discovering new places. To have no obligations, no family, no people. The thought was exhilarating and terrifying. Though she loved her wings and the fantasy of freedom, tears filled her eyes. Venus had given her the keys to her jail cell, but Psyche knew she would not go free.

She forced herself to look at the goddess's face as she answered her question. "I would fly up to the heavens and find my husband."

"My son is not your husband," Venus hissed, her voice echoing through the temple. "Gods do not marry mortals. We bed mortals and give them children, but we do not marry!"

Venus's eyes flashed red as she went behind the girl and caught one wing between her hands, caressing the silken skin, so fragile and thin.

"You are playthings for us, amusing for a time, the way you take your short lives so seriously. The earnestness in which you endeavor to find meaning and comfort can be quite entertaining. But all gods grow tired of mortals, no matter how fervent their love feels in the beginning. All things must come to an end."

And then slowly, delicately, Venus began to pull. Care held Psyche's wrists taut so she could not move. Pleading would do no good, but she could not stop herself from begging as Venus slowly tugged at her wing. Then, in one fluid movement, the goddess tugged until she plucked the wing from Psyche's back and tossed it on the floor. Psyche cried out, tasting her own tears. There was no physical pain, only despair.

Venus took hold of the other wing. "Should I leave you this one?" the goddess asked, laughing. "A memory of what almost was." She rubbed the beautiful blue silk between her thumb and forefinger. "How would you look then? Who would take you to wife with one useless wing? No. I am the Goddess of Love and Beauty. I can't disfigure the most beautiful mortal, can I?" She caressed the wing, sending surges of pleasure through the thin gossamer. "Even if you had wings as strong as my son's, you would never escape Care's hold on you." The goddess laughed and Care chimed in. Her nervous laughter was high-pitched as if she was just being polite.

Venus gave a quick yank, ripping out the second wing. Psyche moaned and went slack in Care's grip.

But the goddess was only beginning her torment. Venus ran her fingertips along Psyche's waist and stroked her haunches. She cupped Psyche's unmarked buttock and pinched her hard.

"Bend her."

Care relaxed her hold on Psyche's wrists and pulled her over so Psyche was in the same humiliating position the God of War had put her in—her hair dangled to the white marble floor, her breasts flopped forward, her buttocks exposed, her nether lips slightly parted. Care let go of her wrists, but Psyche dared not move.

Venus stood behind her, stroking the unmarked side of Psyche's buttocks. With one delicate finger, she teased the crevice. "Are you still a virgin here?" she asked, fingering the puckered orifice. "Perhaps I should call the God of War back to take you like a soldier. That seems a fitting sacrifice for the mortal who dared to call him to my temple."

Psyche could not speak. Venus's finger there filled her with an unexpected yearning. She had never wanted anyone to touch her there. But now she longed for Venus's finger to probe her further. She was horrified by the pleasure she took in imagining Mars taking her from behind, thrusting his giant shaft into her while the goddess and her handmaidens watched. How could she long for him to ravish her like that? Shame burned in her cheeks and chest. She deserved whatever punishment Venus gave her.

"Would you like that, little Psyche? I think you would." She caressed Psyche almost tenderly, assailing her with desire. Unable to stifle a moan, Psyche bit her lip hard. It took all her strength not to drop to her knees and beg the goddess to do it.

"But I do not think I want to see that. Besides, he is busy procuring our son's permission for me to kill you. Until then..." She pinched Psyche's nether lips shut, and moved her hand to the place the God of Love had marked her.

Psyche heard Venus gasp and felt her hand draw away. She could not hear well over the pounding of her heart, but she heard Venus say. "Charmed... Ah, my son might be smarter than I give him credit for." Psyche peeked through her legs and saw the goddess kiss her own palm and rub it on her breast.

"Well, little beast, there is plenty of you I can punish."

The goddess stroked the unmarked side of Psyche's buttocks, then pulled back. With the flat of her hand, she struck the girl hard. Once. Psyche put her hands to the ground to steady herself, and Venus's hand came at her again, bringing stinging pain that left an echo of pleasure. The sound of the goddess's palm against Psyche's flesh filled the temple.

Psyche waited, expecting more blows, but instead the goddess laughed. "I would continue this way, little beast, but I see you enjoy it too much, for whenever I touch you, you nearly swoon. Sorrow, Care, have you ever seen a mortal respond to me this way?" The goddess ran a finger along Psyche's crevice, just as the God of War had. "The girl is so wet, it's as if she's been had by a man." Venus laughed. "Several men." She rubbed Psyche's bud with the tip of her finger and Psyche moaned aloud, wishing to die.

"But it is pain I want to give her, not pleasure." Venus paused, and Psyche opened her eyes, gazing at the goddess from between her legs. Venus lifted a perfectly arched eyebrow at Sorrow and Care and grinned.

"Ah, yes! Loyal handmaidens, I have settled on the perfect punishment for this one. Care, harness all your worries and Sorrow, recall all your regrets. This mortal had the God of Love in her bed every night, and she threw it all away for curiosity.

Ladies, take off your belts and whip her. Perhaps your whips can remove that mark."

Psyche did not dare speak. She dropped to her knees between the discarded butterfly wings. Care unwound the red sash from her waist. Sorrow slowly pulled a black silk sash from her girdle. She did not smile, but the lack of grief on her face was the same as a grin. Venus leaned back in her throne, her eyes aflame.

"Stand up," the goddess commanded. "I want to see you driven to your knees with regret and grief."

Psyche stood on trembling legs. Where was he? She had thought he would save her. He had left her, had promised her severe punishment, but she did not expect this. She had thought he would come by now.

"My son lied to me for you, little beast. He gave you what he has given no woman, and in return, you burned him! No mortal has ever injured a god like this and lived. I should tear your flesh, but instead, I will have my loyal servants tear your heart!"

The first blow from Sorrow's black ribbon felt like a caress. The silk moved over Psyche's back soft as a butterfly kiss. But after penetrating the skin, complete misery overtook her, plunging her heart into a black abyss of suffering. As grief consumed her, Care's red ribbon struck her across the shoulders, soft as a feather, but filling her belly with dread and worry. Then Sorrow's black ribbon whipped her again, reawaking all the pain of her broken heart. The misery of the night he left her came back. She was alone, despised, wretched. There was no reason to live without him, yet he forbade her from taking her own life. Care's red sash struck her lower back. Had he ever cared for her? Did he watch and do nothing to stop this?

She fell to her knees, gasping.

Sorrow lashed her mid-back. She had been given love and had thrown it away. She deserved this. Care whipped her harder, the sash still gentle on her skin, but striking her heart. This was all her fault. If only she had obeyed him as a wife should. Why did she have to light the lamp? Why did she have to look? Sorrow's black ribbon beat her. Regret licked at her, a shadow gobbling her soul.

Psyche cried out, putting her hands on the cold marble floor to keep from falling over.

Venus watched, her eyes alight. "Harder."

Care raised her red sash. It beat down on Psyche's shoulders. The doubt it stirred almost undid her. Had he ever loved her? Perhaps she was only his plaything as Venus had said. Perhaps he had had hundreds of women who he had done the same thing to, told the same lies to, each of them believing they were his wife. That was why he wasn't here. He was with another. He did not spare a single thought for her. And he had been honest all along; he was, indeed, a monster.

"Beg, little beast. I want to hear you plead."

"Please, goddess. Please have mercy!"

Venus's smile had never been so wide. "No," she said. "I don't believe in mercy."

Psyche wept on the ground as Sorrow beat her, pushing her deeper into the chasm of dark pain. She was alone as she would be until the end of her days. There would be no reprieve from her suffering. Care's lash came at her again. This was all her fault, for being beautiful, for drawing his attention, and for disobeying. Sorrow whipped her. She would never see him again, never be held in his arms. Her body would never know joy again, only pain. Care struck her. He watched from the heavens laughing at her torment. He had asked his mother to do this, to avenge the pain she had caused him. Sorrow's black lash licked her buttocks. He had promised to punish her. He relished watching her suffering. Next he would appear and command her to be Venus's sacred whore. Care's red ribbon beat her. It had all been a cruel joke. She was only a plaything of the gods. They all laughed at her now. Perhaps he even had an immortal lover who laughed with him.

Psyche was crushed, dashed, and broken, the most miserable of all creatures—he did not love her, and he never had.

"Please." She moaned, looking not at Venus, or Care and Sorrow, but addressing the heavens. "Please, husband, come back to me!"

Psyche crumbled onto the marble, her breasts cold against the stone. Venus's handmaidens ceased their beating as the mortal's sobs echoed through the temple. Psyche struggled to return from the dark abyss of sorrow. Her only solace was that the bracelet he had given her was still on her left wrist. Wiping her eyes, she raised herself on one hand, daring to glance at Venus. The goddess was no longer amused.

"My son said he did not sink the shaft of his arrow into your heart. I do not understand you, mortal. How can you endure this and still long for him?"

Psyche craned her neck to see what she could of her back. Neither the wings the goddess had given her and ripped out nor the whips that had pained her so seemed to have left any mark on the outside. One side of her buttocks was red where Venus had struck her. The other cheek was pale in comparison, but she could still see the outline of his hand there. He claimed her still. She tried to talk, but her mouth would not move properly. It wasn't possible to answer the goddess without dissolving into tears. She tried twice before finally whispering, "True love endures."

"True love?" Venus said incredulously. "Is my love not true? Love is in the moment. It happens in a flash and then disappears just as quickly as passion is spent. You know nothing, little beast." She smiled suddenly. "Little beast… hmm. Yes. Since I cannot kill you, I will work you like a beast." Turning to her handmaidens she said, "I suppose you should feed her. Then take her to my storehouse and have her sort the grain."

Care and Sorrow each took an arm and pulled her up from the floor. They held her upright before the goddess. Venus looked at her with new eyes. "If you insist on continuing, I will set you a task. Let's see how you do in labors of housewifery. If you can sort all the grain by dawn, I will consider permitting you to see my son. Now, I have no more time to waste with you. I have a wedding to attend."

CHAPTER 8

THE FIRST TASK

Sorrow and Care gave Psyche some brown bread and water, but did not permit her to dress. She shook her hair over her shoulders to cover herself. *When you serve as my priestess, this will be your only gown.* She shuddered, remembering Venus's words and wanted only to drop to the ground and weep. But Care and Sorrow watched her, triumph in their eyes.

Psyche stood up straight. Sorrow and Care would not be allowed to change her love to bitterness and self-pity. She shied away from the touch of their cold hands, as they ushered her behind the temple to a neglected storehouse.

The dirt floor was covered in every kind of grain—barley, millet, oat, and poppy seeds, all mixed together. Care laughed when she saw the task Psyche was to accomplish. This time, her laugh was high and mad, like a dog howling at the moon. "If you want to please my mistress, simply sort that out before the dawn."

"Oh, it is impossible," Sorrow said, a black tear leaking from her eye. She turned to Care. "Poor creature," she whispered, "I almost pity her."

"I am only glad not to be her." Care's high voice responded. "But I suppose we should offer her a little help." She handed

Psyche a lamp, her manic laughter returning. "Here, mortal, now you can see the impossible task that lies before you!"

Care's laughter mixed with Sorrow's which was low and gravely, like an echo coming out of a cave. The two goddesses wrapped their arms around each other's waists and walked off, their laughter ringing in Psyche's ears, making her feel she had already gone mad.

Psyche knelt on the floor and began trying to separate the grain. The pieces were small and hard to see. Soon her back ached and her knees hurt. Her mind tormented her with doubt and the futility of the task before her. She tried to convince herself that the thoughts Care and Sorrow had beaten into her with were not true. Her love was stronger than their torment. Remembering all the nights they had spent together and the secrets they had spoken of in the dark, she tried to convince herself that he would not let his mother kill her.

But despite her resolve, Care and Sorrow's manic laughter echoed in her ears. It was infectious and Psyche too began to laugh. There was no way she could sort the grain before the dawn, or even within the turning of a moon. What would Venus do to her next? The goddess did not expect her to finish this task. Psyche's laughter soon died out, replaced by tears. She raised her eyes to the roof of the temple. "Please, husband, help me. Even if you do not yet forgive me, allow me to see you again. There is something I must tell you."

Using her finger, she drew a bow and arrow and lowered her head, so her tears fell upon the dirt. The hair on the back of her neck stood up and a swarm of ants appeared. She scooted back on her knees, but they came toward her. She backed away further, but a crumpled grain sack tripped her and she fell back onto her buttocks.

The ants came at her, climbing onto her bare leg. She brushed them off. Venus wanted to treat her like a beast. Already naked and dirty, she did not want insects on her. But the ants that had crossed her body began to move the grain, sorting the oats, the barley, and millet. She stared in disbelief. They had come to help her! But they would not do it for free.

In disbelief, she did not move as the colony of ants surged toward her. She clenched her fists and allowed the slow trail of ants to creep over her calf to her thigh. All of her instincts screamed to stand up, to shriek and slap the ants off of her. But she mastered herself. How else would the task be accomplished? The ants that had climbed over her were moving the grain in earnest, separating each so like was with like.

Their tiny feet tormented her with their light touch, like a stray strand of hair that had fallen down her dress. They marched over her skin, delicately winding their way over her leg. The black column trailed over her skin, tickling her until she struggled with herself not to bat them away. She imagined Venus watching her and laughing—except the goddess would not bother to spy.

But her husband was another matter. She raised her eyes to the heavens, picturing his golden eyes, his strong bronzed back, remembering his hands clenched in her hair.

"My love," she said to the sky, "if this is a test of what I am willing to endure for you, I will manage it. This and more if you'll only come back to me."

The torment of the ants was nothing she told herself. Her fear of leaving her family and kingdom to be sacrificed to a monster; the way her husband had looked when the oil burned his skin; the shock of betrayal as he realized he must leave her, how her heart was torn in two as he flew away from her; the suffocating pain of Venus crushing the life out of her; being lashed by Care and Sorrow—all these things were far worse than a colony of ants marching over her leg in order to help her.

Once, when she was a little girl, her sisters had found several peacock feathers left over from a celebration honoring Juno. Iris had held Psyche's arms above her head while Lily tickled her armpits with the feathers. Psyche had laughed at first as the feather brushed her skin, but her sisters had continued until she was crying, promising them whatever they asked. This was how the ants felt now.

Trying not to squirm, she flexed her thigh, hardening the muscle, but she could still feel them. Her hand reached out to brush them off, but she stopped herself. Even with the ants' help it was a tremendous amount of work to do before dawn.

"My love will endure," she said. "True love endures." She repeated, pinching different parts of her body to distract herself.

Even after the ants were off her skin, she could still feel them, the ghost of a caress, an itch she could not scratch. She stood up, rubbing her leg, slapping her thigh and calf. She preferred pain to the slow maddening tickle.

Yet when she lifted the lamp, she saw that the piles of grain were becoming neat and orderly. Her torment was making the impossible possible. Venus's task would be accomplished. The goddess would permit her to see her husband.

And then, overcome from being so close to death at the hands of the gods, she picked up the empty grain sack, and finding another, made herself a bed. Exhaustion overtook her, and she fell into a deep sleep.

CHAPTER 9

YES, THE RIVER KNOWS

Psyche was roused from sleep when the storehouse door was opened. There was a draft of cold air and a shocked silence.

"Which god helped you?" Venus asked, her voice rising like the wind.

Psyche opened her eyes, too drowsy to be scared.

"No gods helped me, goddess."

Venus's eyes shone with an impassioned fury. As clearly as if Venus had spoken, Psyche knew her thoughts—even the smallest creatures were so taken with this mortal's beauty that they wished to help her. Venus's hand shot out and though she did not touch her, Psyche found herself trembling in the dirt.

"Very surprising, mortal. I shall have to set you another task. Perhaps one not quite so easy… hmm. Look at you, disheveled, filthy. Not presentable to me or my son at all. But I have an idea."

Thoughts of a warm bath taunted Psyche. To have her hair combed and washed, to be dressed in fine clothing—or to be dressed in any clothing at all. But Venus's smile put her on guard.

"There are some sheep, golden rams that belong to the sun. To get to them, you need to swim across a river. You can bathe there. If you succeed in getting to the other side, you can begin your second task of gathering wool from the golden rams. Since you are such a dutiful servant, I'm sure it would be your pleasure to collect the golden wool so my handmaidens can spin it into a gown for me. Will you do this for me, Psyche?" The sweetness in her voice was terrifying.

"But," Psyche started. She had done what Venus asked. The grain was sorted. It was not fair to give her another task.

"Truly, little beast, you are not the one who sorted the grain. I think it is only right for you to redeem yourself on your own merit. Do you agree to do as I ask?"

"Yes," Psyche said, seeing no other choice.

Venus snapped her fingers and Psyche found herself sitting upon the dewy grass under the early morning sun. She heard the river before seeing it. The wild water roared through the valley. Fluid with motion, the river flowed with maddened energy. Beyond the water was a pasture where a flock of golden rams nibbled on grass. Wool glittering brightly in the sun, their horns seemed razor sharp even from across the raging river. The wind shifted and she could smell them. Dank, strong, like all sheep except the smell of metal mixed with the wooly smell and iron. They smelled of blood.

Standing on the banks, Psyche gazed at the fearsome current, watching logs and leaves dashed against rocks. Reckless emotion surged in her and she began to weep bitterly. The sorrow and doubt the goddess's handmaidens had sown in her heart would not leave her. She was a fool to go against the goddess! She was lucky Venus had only beaten her and not sent her to serve in her temple, turned her into a hag, or a statue in the God of Love's house. She shuddered at the thought of spending eternity silently watching him.

Even still, there was no way to live without him. She chided herself for her foolishness. Her husband had left her, vowing to punish her with a broken heart. He had abandoned her to his mother's hatred. What was the purpose of this fruitless endeavor?

Why did she pine for him? Risk her life for him? Yet it did not matter what reason said. If she could not have him, she would perish. Let it be by water.

She sat on the banks, her tears falling on the grass. He had forbidden her from taking her own life, but why should she obey him? If he was her husband no longer, then she could do as she wished and end it. Gathering her courage, she prepared to fling herself into the rough current.

"Please," she said to the raging river, "take me quickly. Do not make me suffer much. I have had enough of that now."

Her decision made, she stood. She would disobey her husband and allow the goddess to win. The cold wind blew, caressing her face as she prepared to enter the water. By the gods, she prayed, let it be quick.

But as she moved toward the river, a murky voice rose up through the foam.

"Mortal, your tears called to me and provoked me into creating a form. Now I am aware of you and your suffering. You long to come into me, to end your life inside me. I invite you, come into me, beauty. I will give you not what you think you want, but what you need."

The water god's words slid through her mind, liquid meaning penetrating consciousness. He was the softest thing in the world, yet powerful enough to dash a mighty ship to smithereens. And he spoke the truth; she yearned to be submerged in his depths.

"Thank you, my lord," she said, not completely sure what he meant, but glad that he had heard her.

The cold mud squished between her toes as she went to him. The river was like ice, and a cold wind blew against her naked skin. Her whole body broke into gooseflesh as the current lapped against her feet. All the tiny hairs on her body rose, and her nipples hardened.

"I will warm myself for you," the river god said.

She stepped in deeper, to her ankles, to her calves. The waves slapped at her gently. Though the strength of the river frightened her, she was exhilarated by his power and longed to surrender her body to the current. She cautiously waded in, planting her feet firmly on the muddy bottom, until the water came to her thighs and surrounded her hips. The force of the current could easily sweep her off her feet.

When her pubis touched the river, the water around her body began to warm. The strong flow slowed but still buzzed with currents, rushing against her thighs, moving upwards toward her sex. The pressure of the water caressed her with its gentle force. She tried to stand still in the torrent of streams, but the water pushed her legs apart.

"Come," the river god said, "come into me deeper."

She looked down at her pale belly, just touching the foamy water. Her hard nipples were rosy with cold. The river god wanted her to submerge them into him, but she was not ready to be completely immersed in him yet.

"I want to stay true to my husband."

"Why?" the river god asked, slipping the question into her mind. Foam swirled around her, encircling her waist, slapping at her. Hard water coursed between her legs. "He has left you to the wolves, child. But I do not want to hurt you." The water caressed her buttocks, gently sliding over them, around them, and then with a wave, a stream of water slid into her crevice. "I want to help you, beauty, and I ask only that you come inside me, so I can whisper the secret in your ear."

She feared entering deeper, but deeper she went. Her areolas puckered with cold, but she slipped them into the waiting river. The water lapped at her nipples, bringing her unexpected plea-sure. She stepped in to her shoulders, suddenly losing her foot-ing. The water thrust her away from higher ground, until she floated into the bumpy flow, to the middle of the river. Her feet kicked, trying to find purchase, but the water was too deep. She flailed her arms and legs wildly, having never learned to swim.

This would be her death. Yet the river god held her, cupping her from below and supporting her so her head was above the rough foam.

The water caressed her, washing over her erect nipples and swarming over her belly, moving in waves down her pubis, and trickling inside her where it stroked her and stoked her desire, reminding her of the secrets her husband had taught her in the dark. She felt herself moisten with her own need.

"Wet," the river god whispered. "Feel how wet you are. Touch yourself for me. Open yourself to me."

Desire and curiosity overtook her. She delved her finger into her honey hair, exploring herself as the river carried her. She was slick with yearning. As she caressed herself, the water surged inside her, slapping her gently. The water around her nipples hardened, pulling at her urgently. She stroked herself as her husband had taught her. She had forgotten how good it felt.

Warm liquid pushed against her as she opened herself and rubbed her bud, silken and hard. But she wanted more. The river rushed over her, spreading her wide and invading every part of her while her fingers worked her own pleasure. Her moans were taken by the sound of the water gushing around her.

"Yes," the river god said. "Let me in."

She did as he said, opening herself to him as she continued to stroke herself. The water pounded into her with a mighty force. She pulled her hand away, surrendering to the river. Her arms and legs floated free in the wild water as her heart pounded with desire.

"Take a deep breath, lover," the river god whispered. "I'm going to take you under."

She gasped in fear and excitement as he sucked her into him completely. Immersed in his murky depths, she opened her eyes, seeing nothing except her hair flowing around her. The river god entered her, filling her completely. She resisted the urge to gasp as the river god pounded wave after wave into her. She let him spread her legs wider, opening herself to him as he cleansed her with his swift, pure flow. The bubbles from the last of her breath floated up to the surface, and she wondered if he would release her or keep her forever in his dark embrace. She told herself she did not care. It did not matter if she lived or died.

But then he let her go. Her head popped up to the surface. She sucked in the air, taking it deep into her lungs. The river grew hot and froth shot up around her. She sighed, relaxing into him, and he held her up.

Psyche floated for a moment in complete contentment. She gazed up into the sky. The sun had risen fully and a few puffy clouds sat low on the horizon. The trees had lost most of their leaves, and the grass on the banks was turning brown. But the sky was blue, and she was still alive.

"I will tell you the secret," the water lapped at her ear. "The golden rams yearn for human flesh. If you approach them, they will skewer you with their golden horns. They will hold you down while the others eat your skin and your screams reach the heavens. They like their victims to beg for death and only then will they gore you in the heart.

"However, if you wait for the sun to rise high in the sky, they will move away from the river into the shade of the trees. Then you can easily gather their wool from the brambles. Wait just a little longer. When you want to cross back, I will slow my current for you, my beauty."

This was the death Venus wanted for her, not to be stabbed once, but many times. To beg for death. And she had just told herself Venus had been merciful. She would not make this mistake again.

"You are so kind, my lord. Why do you help me?" He could easily drown her now.

"You asked me to take you, beauty, both your body and your life. When a mortal offers her life, it is the godly thing to give it back with a reason for living. It is my pleasure to have you inside me, and for me to be inside you." The water seemed to grip her tightly for a moment, but Psyche did not struggle against him.

"Besides, it has been so long since a mortal has heard me, and even longer since I have had a woman."

"You have saved my life, my lord, like a true god. I will always be indebted to you."

The water around her warmed more, and she let herself float in his gentle embrace. The river god would not let her drown, even if she wanted to. And it was not because he feared her husband. It was not even because she was beautiful. She knew then without a doubt that the gods had given her a gift that went beyond physical beauty. For the first time since her love left her, she smiled.

She had not meant to sleep, but the river rocked her so gently. When she opened her eyes, the great god Pan was perched on a rock watching her. The wind shifted, filling her nostrils with his goaty scent, different from the metallic-wooly smell of the golden rams. His goat legs were matted with thick, brown fur, but his arms and chest were strong like a shepherd's. His eyes were the color of wheat. The rectangular pupils gazed at her, and he grinned as she looked at him with recognition.

"Princess," he said in a throaty voice, "we all you want you to succeed. Do not be deterred. You will persevere."

The river rocked her gently but a choppy wave splashed her face, upsetting her balance. She stopped floating, her ears full of water and her eyes wet. She looked back to the rock, but the god of wild things was gone.

As the sun moved over the pasture, the rams did as the river god had said and went far away into the shade. Psyche could see their golden wool glistening in the branches. After getting out of the water, she gathered her hair in her hands and wrung it out upon the grass. The cold wind chilled her and she wished for a cloak. She scrambled up the banks to the pasture and began plucking the wool from the bushes. Among the brambles, she found a piece of faded brown cloth. On the ground were the bones of the last mortal who had come for the golden rams. With a trembling hand, she pulled the fabric free and used it to hold the golden tufts.

When she returned to the river, she held the wool up, safe and dry in the cloth. The river god again slowed his current and warmed the water around her body. She thanked him again for his kindness, but he just slapped quietly at her skin as she climbed onto the banks. Once she left his warmth, she shivered in earnest. The days were growing short and cold. At this time of year, her nurse Diana always said that Proserpina would soon go to Hades and Ceres would punish the earth with winter.

She looked up to the skies, searching for her love, seeing only his mother's star. Was he watching her? Did he know how she had suffered for him? Sudden fear overtook her. Had he seen what she had done with the river god? Thinking of the river god's words rekindled the doubt Care had beat into her. Had her husband abandoned her? Had he forgotten about her? Had he never loved her at all?

But she did not believe it. She just did not understand why he did not come.

Venus appeared with the sunset on the other side of the river, searching for Psyche's broken body. Unable to see the girl, she put her hands out, casting about to feel her beating heart. Her head turned sharply, and she saw Psyche across the banks where she had left her.

In a flash, Venus was standing above her.

"Little beast, have you been here all day? Too afraid to cross the river for me?"

"No, goddess. I have done what you commanded. The wool is here." She offered Venus the sack. The goddess's eyes grew wide in rage. There was even enough golden wool to spin a short gown.

"All wrapped tightly in the cloak of a dead man. How nice. Who helped you?"

Psyche cast her eyes down. Could Venus punish the river? But she knew the goddess would hurt her until she told. Venus reached her white hand toward Psyche, her fingertips gently brushing her throat. The vibrations of pleasure began to hum, but before those fingers could grab her, Psyche pulled away and cried, "It was the river. The river slowed his current to allow me to the other side. I gathered the wool myself. Please, goddess, I have done what you asked! Please let me see my husband!"

The goddess's fingers reached out and stroked Psyche's throat almost tenderly.

"You have been very dutiful, child. So obedient to me though not to my son. I believe there was only one thing he required of you. But you were too curious to obey, weren't you? And your curiosity will be your undoing in the end." Venus gripped Psyche's arm tightly. "Come, I will take you back to my palace. I suppose I should feed you again, perhaps even allow you to dress. Tomorrow I will decide what to do with you."

CHAPTER 10

IN VENUS'S PALACE

The next thing Psyche knew, she was no longer by the river. Before her stood Venus's home in the clouds of Olympus. Built of pink marble with columns adorned with gold, Venus's cloud-shrouded abode trumped anything that could be built on earth.

Realizing she was alone, Psyche took a deep breath and smelled jasmine and roses. The air itself was pure and sweet like the morning after a spring rain. The only sounds were of fountains and birdsong. Surrounded by pink clouds and the darkening sky, she felt suddenly lazy, as if there were no better way to spend her time than to find a lover and retire to bed. Somewhere inside this building was her husband. She shook her tangled hair over her shoulders and moved toward the atrium.

Orange eyes aflame, Care stepped out of the shadows. The creases of her face vanished as she grinned.

"The disobedient servant. Come, mortal. I will take you to the slave quarters."

Psyche followed Venus's handmaiden down pink marble stairs, trying not to gape. Venus's slave quarters were still more lavish than most palaces on earth. The ceilings were twice as tall as the tallest man. The walls were painted with frescos of the arts of love and images of roses and doves adorned the high ceilings.

"Please," Psyche said as Care turned to leave, "may I have something to wear?"

"Why? Do you worry what others will think of your body? That they will find fault with your big breasts or whisper to each other that truly you are no beauty."

Care's words wove their magic of worry. Vain fear overtook Psyche. She had been called the second coming of Venus, and now here in the goddess's palace, all her servants would see it was not true. Her body was not as it had been. Her breasts had swelled, her belly was no longer flat, her arms and legs were much too thin. She was a mortal among goddesses, a nag among purebreds.

Delight shone in Care's eyes. "Yes," she said, "naked mortal, everyone will see how you really are. Do you wish to cover up the strange discoloration of your skin? Do you worry they will see a handprint on your buttock and know how you rutted about in the light of day, no better than a whore?"

For a moment, it worked. The terror of being thought of as an indecent woman overwhelmed her. Images of beautiful immortals laughing and calling her names filled her mind. But clutching the wedding band on her wrist, Psyche returned to herself. She was not a whore. She had been faithful to one man. Her love was pure and true.

"No," she said to Care. "I am proud of that mark. It means my husband claims me still. I asked for clothing because I am cold and would like to cover myself." She hoped the first part of what she said was true. Yet, just as she had believed her shadow husband was the winged one, she would continue to believe he loved her still. After speaking, she realized that it was neither cold nor hot in Venus's palace. In fact, there seemed to be no temperature at all.

Care seemed amused by Psyche's resistance. "Would you like

to wear my mantle?" she asked, pulling a red scarf from her shoulders. "I can wrap you in woe and worry and clothe you in fear and regret. Did my sister Sorrow and I not give you enough already? I would be happy to give you more, for truly I felt unburdened after beating you, little Psyche." Care began to unknot more of her multicolored strands. "In fact," she whispered, "why don't you take all of these and I will walk the halls naked, not worrying about anything."

"No!" Psyche said, taking a step back.

Care laughed for a moment, then the lines of apprehension creased her brow once more.

"Then I will leave you as you are and remain as I am, each with worries of our own."

Left alone in a corridor, Psyche looked about her. Exquisite carpets lay over the marble. There were couches placed along the hallway, as if every inch of Venus's palace was designed for an unexpected tryst.

Soon she heard voices of other immortals. "Yes, Care said she's down here." A demigoddess wearing a wreath of primroses in her hair and a green dryad approached.

"Look at her," the demigoddess said. "Beautiful still, but I'd rather have my own looks than inspire the goddess's anger as she has."

"Yes." The dryad agreed, staring at Psyche with her bright green eyes. "I thank the Fates we do not share her lot. Though," she whispered to her friend, "imagine sharing your bed with the God of Love, and I heard he shared it with her nightly!"

The demigoddess laughed. "Yet she was not satisfied with his affections. The ungrateful mortal burned him with oil."

"Is he here?" Psyche asked. "My husband, the God of Love, is he here?"

The two stared at her for a moment, as if she were a child who had spoken out of turn.

"Please," Psyche said, as they began to turn away.

"'*Please*,'" the demigoddess mocked, her voice a perfect imitation of Psyche's. "Yes, I've heard how you can beg, little vixen." She turned her attention back to her friend. "Were you there when Care recounted how she and Sorrow made the little bitch beg? '*Please*,'" she said again. "What do you think, mortal, that he will come for you here, in his mother's palace?" Turning back to her friend, she dissolved in laughter.

"Oh," the dryad said, a note of pity in her voice, as she wiped a tear from her eye, "he must have shot her so hard! The girl has no sense. He is a monster, isn't he?"

"Yes," the other replied, her laughter dying down. She lowered her voice and said. "But if he came to my bed, I would not ask him to leave!"

Undeterred, Psyche continued to query the minor goddesses and dryads who passed by. Most ignored her, but a once been beautiful naiad, with sea-green eyes and hair the color of a peacock feather brought Psyche a basket of barley cakes sweetened with honey.

"Thank you," Psyche said. The blue naiad wordlessly handed her a cup of wine, which she drank gratefully.

"I am grateful for your kindness," Psyche said. "Do you know where my husband is?"

The blue naiad stared back in response, but did not speak. An autumn-hued dryad walked by with a basket of roses. Looking at Psyche and the naiad, she smirked.

"She can't answer you. Our mistress ripped out her tongue for gossiping about her. What do you think she'll do to you, mortal?" The dryad giggled, her laughter like dry leaves rustling in the trees as she walked away.

The blue naiad stared at Psyche and cast her gaze upward for a brief moment. Then she looked at Psyche meaningfully. Her husband was in the rooms above!

"Can you take me to him?" Psyche whispered. But the naiad's

sea blue eyes grew wide in terror. She backed away slowly, seeming to disappear into the shadows.

But her love was near, and Venus had not killed her yet. He must know she was here. Perhaps he would come while she slept.

She found a couch and lay down, glad to have a full belly. Exhaustion overtook her and she fell into a happy dream that they were back in his palace. He was her shadow husband, only his golden eyes glowed in the darkness as they exchanged secrets of their souls. In her dreams, he took her back and forgave her.

But she awoke to find Venus staring down at her flanked by Care and Sorrow. Care absentmindedly fingered her red sash. Sorrow used her black ribbon to wipe her eyes. Yet Venus had never been more beautiful. Her long, golden tresses were perfectly coifed in the most stylish chignon. The pearly white skin of her breasts was visible between the folds of her golden gown. Psyche wanted more than ever to please the goddess. Barely able to stop herself from kneeling at the goddess's feet, Psyche realized Venus was wearing her magic girdle, embroidered with doves and full of amorous magic.

"Do you still wish to see my son, little beast?"

"Yes, goddess, more than anything," Psyche said standing up.

"Alas, he is still recovering from his wound. You have hurt him deeply. If you really want to see him, I will give you another task. Or perhaps instead, I shall set you free."

"No, goddess, I must see him."

Venus stared at Psyche, studying her. Then she turned to her handmaidens, "Look at this girl and rejoice in your immortality. Behold the tragedy of being a mortal woman; their beauty is so fleeting. One day in the sun, age, the woes of a mortal life… And this one has ceased to care for herself; her skin is wan, her hair unbrushed. And you know what the baby will do to her…" She plunged her hand into Psyche's hair, pulling it roughly. Psyche shuddered, but knew better than to shy away. Venus put a hand on Psyche's breast and moved down to her ribs.

"So skinny, little beast. You should be filling out now. You should be lying on a silken couch, drinking milk and honey, eating roasted meat and fish fresh from the sea, fruit from the garden from your mortal husband's trees.

"You were a princess once. Where are your jewels and your fine gowns? Only this one bangle on your wrist and an emerald around your neck. Your skin is dry and discolored. You don't have a single slave. All this for your confused idea of love." The goddess's face darkened. Psyche knew to be worried as Venus ran her hand to Psyche's back, feeling the flesh of her buttocks, bringing pleasure to every place she touched, even when she pinched her skin.

"I know what love is, little beast. Love is carnal. It is the urgent need to put your hands on your lover's body. It comes in a flash, like a fever, and then it is gone. Love does not care if the beloved is married or loves another, for my love is in the moment. It is the profile of a stranger seen beneath the olive trees, the flash of a muscular thigh under a tunic. Love is many things, but it is not this thing you go on about, long-lasting and all-enduring." She moved her hand to Psyche's pubis, sliding her finger into Psyche's honey hair.

"This is how love feels," Venus said, stroking her. "I hate you, yet I can make you wish to worship me with your last breath." The goddess teased her for a moment while looking deep into her eyes. The goddess's eyes were now golden like her son's, and Psyche was momentarily lost, remembering the moment love had first struck her.

Venus's full red lips spread in a grin. The goddess's finger wriggled against her, probing until she was right against the girl's bud. Psyche's breath came hard, gasping at the pleasure surging through her. Hardly able to stand, she tried to resist, to refuse Venus. But the sensation of the goddess's hard finger against her throbbing sex, sent bolts of pleasure that would not be denied.

Psyche moaned despite herself. Venus smiled and withdrew her hand, allowing the mortal to fall to her knees.

"Perhaps I should make you worship me until your last breath, little beast. Hmmm?" She raised her hand to Psyche, who could only cower and back away. She could too easily imagine how the goddess would kill her, making her come into her pleasure again and again until she could bear it no longer.

"No," Psyche whispered.

The goddess laughed with glee. "My son foreswore you, and yet you traipse all over the Empire, weeping for him, begging to see him. What claim do you have on the God of Love? How dare you call him husband! There was no real wedding!" She glanced at Psyche dismissively.

"His child grows in your belly. So? You are not the first woman in this situation. Find another man to raise it or leave it for the wild beasts. My son does not want you! And I grow tired of keeping you. I am weary of hearing what you think love is when I, the Goddess of Love, know better than anyone!"

Psyche knelt on the ground gasping. Care put her hand on the girl's shoulder, filling her with doubt. The goddess was right. Clearly, he no longer wanted her. He had told her so himself and had not come to her aid. Venus had almost strangled Psyche, beaten her, and sent her to be killed by the river and the golden rams, and he had not come.

Yet his handprint remained outlined on her body, his wedding band stayed on her wrist. The God of War had said her husband would love her until that mark faded. Venus had not killed her. She crawled away from Care's hand, grateful for the strength of the marble beneath her knees and palms.

"I offer you once last chance, mortal; go back to your father. He will take you. Men will line up to have you as a wife even with a pup in your belly. You can spend the next seven months lying on a couch, drinking milk and honey, eating whatever you desire, served by slaves. You will forget my son. The pain will dull. You will have a fine life, learn to love your new husband and his gold. It may not be the *love* you go on about, but it will be a life for you and your child. Come now, what do you say?"

Psyche did not know what Venus would do if she refused. None who had crossed the goddess had lived on as a mortal. All had become mute things, trees, stones, plants. But she could not give up. She would continue until she saw her husband again or Venus killed her.

Psyche stayed on her knees, but lifted her hands from the ground. She knelt straight up, looking into the goddess's eyes which seemed to darken.

It took all of Psyche's courage to speak and her voice, barely above a whisper, trembled.

"I will perform another task for you, goddess, if you will only let me see him again."

Venus smiled wryly. "Ah, little beast, well, it must be said that you do not disappoint, and you have been rather entertaining. What I require of you now is a heroic task, not one for a mere girl, a princess." She smiled at Care and Sorrow who delighted in the shared joke. "Tending to my son and dealing with you has diminished my beauty. My last task for you is to go to the Underworld and bring me back some beauty from the Queen of the Dead."

Hades! No mortal could go to Hades and return alive. Only heroes had gone—Odysseus, Hercules, Theseus, Orpheus, and Aeneas. Orpheus had gone for love and returned brokenhearted. She shuddered, imagining his head floating away from his body down the river.

"You grow pale, little Psyche. This should be no problem for you. You have been so successful in your other tasks. I will even deliver you to the mouth of the Underworld myself." Venus touched her almost gently. "Do this for me and I swear by the River Styx, if you return, I will permit you to see my son."

Renewed by this promise, Psyche pushed her fear away. "Goddess, before I go, may I please have some clothing and some bread to take on my journey? And a coin, no, two coins for Charon?"

Venus turned to Care and Sorrow and laughed. "Of course, dear girl. We will be sure to feed you and give you food for your journey, a new gown even. Care will give you all you ask."

Care and Sorrow took her to the slaves' bath, fed her, and clothed her in a dusky rose gown, which Sorrow said brought out the color in her cheeks. Care gave her everything she asked for, but Psyche worried she had not requested the right things. She had only asked for bread and barley cakes, coins, a bladder full of water, a gray traveling cloak, and a pouch to keep everything in.

Soon Venus came and snapped her fingers. Before Psyche realized what was happening, she was standing at the mouth of Hades, alone. *I will die*, she thought and then laughed. Dying was what mortals did before going to Hades. But then she remembered the great god Pan. He said they all supported her. Ceres had wanted to help her, Mars, the ants, the river god. How far she had come, from a frightened girl waiting to be eaten by a monster to a woman who was choosing to go to the Underworld with the hope of returning. She put her hand on her buttocks, feeling the place her husband had marked her, and pretended she was holding his hand.

CHAPTER 11

INTO THE UNDERWORLD

The descent was not steep, but dark and quiet. Psyche made her way down carefully, wrapped in her traveling cloak. Soon she began to see shades drifting about. They were hardly more than shadows wearing the memories of faces, enshrouded by a quiet sorrow. An icy claw of fear gripped her belly. She was among the dead! Quelling her panic, she reminded herself that they could not hurt her unless they changed places with her.

Her sister Iris had loved tales of the Underworld and on cold winter nights had asked their nurse Diana for them. Psyche had been frightened at the time, but now, the stories came back to her —Charon the ferryman would take no one across without a coin, she had to beware of Cerberus, the triple-headed beast with the heads of a dog and tail of a dragon, and above all, she must eat nothing from the Underworld or sit in the seats of the queen and king.

As she continued her descent, she was joined by more and more shades. Weak of limb, weak of mind, Diana had always said. The dead were not aware of her or of themselves. It was only through thoughtless instinct that they were drawn to the River Styx, as a moth is to a flame.

Without sunlight, there was no color. Everything was shrouded in mist—gray, black, brown or white. Though it had not actually been a long time, even a brief time under the earth felt eternal.

Determined, Psyche continued her descent until she came to a man struggling with his donkey cart.

"Please, help me. I only need a little push."

Psyche went toward him and stopped suddenly. She could assist no one, change nothing. Helping another could only be done at her own peril. Turning back she followed the shades down the hill to the river, ignoring the pleas for help that followed her.

The sound of the river reached her. Though it had a mighty current, it did not roar. This was a quiet, still place. The water moved, the river sang, but softly, secretly. Mortal ears were not meant to hear the sound of the River Styx.

Along the way, three women sat weaving, a maiden, a woman in her prime, and a crone.

"Daughter," the old woman said, "come sit with us and rest your weary bones. We will tell you a tale while we spin."

A longing to come near and see what they were spinning pulled her toward them. Just a quick look—she would not sit down. The tapestry was wondrous even from afar. It seemed to glitter with stars and shine with the light of the sun. Like a great web, the three women wove the tapestry. Stepping closer, Psyche could pick out her own thread, shining and golden, like her beloved's eyes. She could almost make out the images of him picking her up on the beach, making love to her in the dark, and leaving her. The strands that represented the gods glittered like diamonds. A pink light shone near her own life—Venus! Psyche took a step back. She would go no closer. The three Fates would cut the thread of her life if she did.

"Forgive me, mother," Psyche said, "I must be on my way."

"Yes," the crone cackled. "On your way indeed. The King and

Queen of the Underworld await you, child." The maiden and the woman began to laugh, too, not bothering to look up from their work.

Shaken, Psyche continued to the river. On the banks, countless shades stood about. Lost were those not buried with a coin in their mouths or those whose corpses had gone unburied. A deep fear began to eat at her thinking of their eternal doom. If she died here, would her corpse be unburied, or would her shade continue, her body and soul entombed in Hades?

She followed the throng to the dock to await Charon. He soon came, standing tall on the prow of his boat, poling his way through the strong current. An ancient god, toiling away for all eternity. His gray cloak was thin as a moth's wing. He was strong and he was bitter. Though he was old, his face long and haggard, the muscles of his chest and back were firm.

The shades approached him, each one opening his or her mouth for him to pull out the coin that had accompanied them in death. Psyche stood among them, her heart pounding. This was the first step toward entering the Underworld. If he denied her, there was no hope in accomplishing her task. She slipped the coin from her bodice and placed it in her mouth, hoping he did not see. But she realized he would easily know that she did not belong. Even hidden by her cloak, all the shades were gray, wisplike, almost transparent, while she was clearly flesh and blood. Her heart pounded so loudly in her ears she was sure all could hear.

"A living creature in the realm of the dead," Charon said, taking the coin from her mouth. His cold fingers caressed her lips. "You seem to have lost your way."

"Lord Charon, I come on an errand from the Goddess of Love and Beauty. She asked me to retrieve something from the Queen of the Underworld."

"The living are not allowed in my king's realm. I have been punished for it before. The last time I let a living being into King

Pluto's realm, he chained me to a wall and beat me until my flesh fell like ribbons upon the ground for Cerberus to lap up."

Perhaps it was better if she turned back now. She wanted to scramble back up the hill, back into the light, into the land of the living. Every cell in her body knew she should not be in the realm of Pluto, the all-seeing invisible king. But she would not be undone by fear.

"But I am no hero. I am only a woman. I make no secret of my coming. I will speak to the queen only if the king wills it. If he does not, I will leave here… or not, as he chooses." She shuddered at the thought and then shuddered again as Charon slipped a bony hand beneath her cloak.

"Let me feel your beating heart," he said, placing the flat of his palm on her chest. She stayed still, realizing that his hand was not cold. In fact, it had no temperature at all. He closed his eyes and inhaled deeply.

"Ah, the smell of a living woman. The feel of the flesh of a living woman. It has been so long, so very long." Opening his eyes, he stared into her face. "I will allow you to board if you open your *stola* and reveal your breasts. It will be worth any punishment if I can look at them as I pole my ferry to Hades."

Psyche tried to swallow, but her mouth was too dry. She was at the ferryman's mercy. Whatever he asked, she would need to do if she wanted to reach the other side.

"But when you take me back," she said, "let me keep them hidden."

He grinned wide, and she could guess that he expected no return trip for her.

"Step aboard, live one."

He took no more passengers and ignored the ten shades that had come before her. After leading her to the center of his boat, he stood waiting for her to pull down her *stola*. She unpinned the sleeves and let the fabric slide to her navel.

"Yes," he said, firmly gripping his pole and standing so he

could watch her as he dug his pole into the soft mud of the River Styx.

As the boat moved, Psyche realized that there was no temperature here. She had expected to be cold, but she was not. It was neither hot nor cold, humid nor dry. There was little wind on the river. Even moving on the water, there was barely a breeze. The silence and stillness surrounded her. There were shades on the banks and even floating listlessly in the gray foam of the river. Some of the shades moaned, but the sound was so soft, easy to dismiss.

Still her nipples grew hard. Charon's nostrils flared and he closed his eyes momentarily, savoring the scent and the sight of her. His strong arms stroked the pole into the water, pushing harder but she noted, not faster. He was in no rush.

"I do this for you, husband," she whispered to herself. "I suffer this for you."

It seemed endless, and Charon's gaze made her feel she was trapped with him in eternal limbo, somewhere between the shore and Hades proper. His gray eyes glowed like embers the longer he stared at her. It seemed that perhaps he could burn with passion and consume her. She fought the urge to pull up her *stola*, to cover her breasts with her hands. This was one of the many prices she would pay to get back the love she had squandered.

Eventually they reached the banks of the realm of the King of the Underworld. Quickly, Psyche pulled up her gown. She was shamed by what Charon had made her do, but she had arrived. The ferryman approached her, giving her a hand to step off.

"May the gods be with you, live one," he said, his laughter like chalk crumbling.

Like all who had come before her, Psyche approached Cerberus. The tripled-headed black beast cocked a head, three pairs of nostrils sniffing furiously at the scent of a living being. When his red eyes lit upon her, she froze in terror. One head raised a rubbery upper lip, revealing razor-sharp steel teeth. The second head growled low, and the third head was silent, waiting to spring. All three heads would eat her alive, tear her to pieces as they each fought for a bite. She roused herself from her stupor and dug into her pouch, procuring a honeyed barley cake. Taking careful aim with her shaking hand, she threw it far. The monster ran for it. As all three heads snapped at each other, she made a mad dash into the Underworld.

Unable to run any farther, Psyche slowed down, reminding herself of the thick chain around the beast's neck. A road paved with bones stood before her. Coming first to the Asphodel Fields, she passed the shades of cheerless heroes, waiting only for the living to pour libations of wine or blood to remember them. Not wanting to remind them of the pleasures of the living flesh, she walked by quickly. She passed a meadow, covered in mist and continued to Erebus. At the end of the road, stood a great palace made of giant bones, gray and strong as granite.

The palace of the God and Goddess of the Underworld seemed unguarded. Psyche approached, but no one came to receive her. It did not seem right to call out in such a silent place. The great hall appeared empty. The floors were silver, bringing a shimmering light into the darkness. Every precious metal and stone beneath the earth belonged to the Lord of the Dead, and his palace showed his riches.

The great thrones stood before her. Empty. The king's throne was a giant black diamond carved into a seat. Light seemed to glow from within. Gold coins littered the floor. The queen's throne was a white diamond with a purple velvet cushion. Butterflies had been trapped within the rock, frozen in time.

"Hello?" Psyche whispered, "Mistress?" She had been taught to never speak the name of the Queen of the Underworld though she wondered what harm it could do her here.

There was no response, only a cold silence. A strong sense of power permeated the air behind her, and she turned quickly. No one was there, but the feeling was so intense that she protectively put a hand on her belly.

Suddenly the King of the Underworld stood before her, pulling off his helm of invisibility to reveal himself. Pluto was older than the other gods. He stared down at her, confident of his complete domination of his realm. Rings adorned every finger—gold, silver, and iron encrusted with diamonds, rubies, lapis lazuli, and sapphires. There were countless gold chains around his neck. His crown shone brightly in a mass of wild black locks, and his pointy black beard blended into his black robes glittering with diamonds. His cold stare froze her to the ground.

"A living woman in my realm," he said, his voice as deep as the earth, "and one bearing fruit."

Psyche quivered as his silver eyes examined her body. Mars had emanated the desire to kill, but Pluto only gave off the feeling of emptiness and permanence. There was no point resisting him. He possessed frightening patience, for all he had to do was wait and every mortal would be his. Psyche sensed it was seldom he was aroused to desire anything but, at that moment, he desired her.

He raised a bushy eyebrow. "I've been waiting for you, Psyche. You've escaped my embrace on numerous occasions, but I have often been on your mind. It seems in your sorrow you have often yearned to enter my realm. And now you have come with your still-beating heart." His voice was like gravel shifting from one palm to another.

He raised his hand, his palm toward her. Pulled by an unstoppable force, Psyche began to walk toward him. She was not sure if he would pluck her heart from her breast or keep her alive for his own pleasure. All she knew was that she feared him more than anything, but she could not stop herself from going to him.

But then a voice like a bird singing on a summer morn broke the spell. "Husband, she has come here for me. Leave her be now. She is mine."

Psyche turned to find Proserpina, stately and cold. Like Psyche, her beauty had been a curse instead of a blessing. Despite her sorrow, the Queen of the Dead was magnificent. Grateful that her feet no longer moved toward King Pluto, Psyche stood still, taking in the majesty of his queen.

Proserpina's dark purple gown glittered with jewels. Her skin was pale as the moon, and her eyes were brown as the earth, like her mother's. The golden crown perched on her flowing black locks seemed more like a manacle than an honor. The sadness that hung about her made Psyche's heart ache. The Queen of the Dead seemed untouchable, but she surprised Psyche by taking her hand and saying, "Come, little mother. Let us go to my boudoir to get what you have come for."

Psyche turned back to the King of the Dead, her heart hammering in her chest. He cocked his head slightly, as if he could hear it.

Though her voice shook, she forced herself to speak. "It's true what you say, All-Seeing King, I would have come sooner, but my husband forbade it. He does not want me dead, but to live with my broken heart." She looked into the abyss of his eyes and quickly away.

As Proserpina led her out of the throne room, she heard a sound like rocks breaking, the sound of his laughter. Psyche clutched her belly, wondering if her fear would dislodge the child in her womb.

But Proserpina's hand held hers tightly. "Calm yourself, little mother. My husband won't hurt you now."

No, Psyche thought, he would not hurt her now—he would hurt her later. There would be no denying the King of the Dead.

Proserpina led Psyche up stairs made of black rock and giants' bones to the women's quarters. The chamber would have been grand, had it not been so dreary. Darkness hid in every corner, shadows of somber solitude. The room was strangely illuminated by glass jars of light, the kind of which Psyche had never seen before.

The shade of a servant soon appeared, awaiting orders.

"What would you like to eat, little mother?" Proserpina asked.

"Thank you, Mistress, I need nothing to eat or drink."

"Come, Psyche. You have had a long, arduous journey. You have nothing to fear from me, for you are my guest. I hope you will stay a while and relax with me."

"Yes, Mistress," Psyche said, looking into Proserpina's brown eyes. The loneliness there almost made her weep. The goddess did not want to hurt her, but she wanted Psyche to stay, possibly even contrive a way to get Psyche to take her place.

"Mistress, may I ask what these lamps are? I've never seen light of this quality before."

"Ah, yes. It is the soul of two lovers connected. When they are reunited, they make this glow. I like to warm my rooms with it, though there is really no warmth here, nor cold. My husband prefers to light his rooms with another kind of lamp. He entwines the souls of those who are judged for punishment with their bitterest enemies. They burn red in their hatred and misery. But I prefer this white light, though it is nothing like the sun..." The Queen of the Underworld seemed to drift away for a moment, then focused her eyes on her guest.

"But you are no stranger to love. Even I have heard of your trials." Proserpina sat on a couch made of rose quartz covered with red cushions. The goddess took Psyche's hands. "Tell me, little mother, why do you do it? I would give anything for my husband to leave me. Yet you have suffered greatly for the mere chance of seeing yours again. Is it true that he did not shoot you with his arrows? That the love comes from you? How can this be? Come, sit next to me and tell me all."

Psyche hesitated, remembering that eating, drinking, or sitting in Proserpina's seat, would lead to an eternity in Hades. She bowed her head and knelt on the ground before the queen.

"Forgive me, Mistress, I must rest for a moment." She was suddenly so very tired. How nice it would be to have a hot cup of wine with honeyed cakes and lie down. The lamps burned bright with trapped souls, shining with love. Love. The Queen of the Dead held her hand still. Psyche noticed the large rings on the queen's fingers, her wedding bracelet of gold and rubies— nothing more than exquisite fetters.

Psyche looked at her own wedding band and remembered the goddess's question.

"There is no reason to what I have done, Mistress. Reason it seems does not often accompany love. All I know is that I did not know what it was to be alive until I met my husband. Even in the dark, he saw me more clearly than anyone.

"Truly, he is the only one who has ever known me—who has ever wanted to know me. Others see only a beautiful face, a fine head of hair, voluptuous breasts, an enticing figure." Psyche paused. Proserpina too had all these attributes. "Though my husband was drawn to my beauty, he wanted to know my soul. By not letting me see him, we saw each other in a way others couldn't… And, he was kind to me. He did not misuse me the way some men do."

She thought suddenly with longing of the things he had done with his hands and tongue. His body against hers, every time different, the way he unlocked hidden pleasure within her. She blushed. Proserpina's face told Psyche she had said too much. It was easy to imagine how the King of the Underworld was in the bedchamber, cold and rough, taking his pleasure from forcing himself on his unwilling wife.

"Forgive me, Mistress, I did not mean… I shouldn't have…."

But Proserpina only looked tragically beautiful, an exotic animal in a cage.

"What is it like to have pleasure?" Proserpina asked, lifting her dark purple gown to expose her pale thighs and the glittering black hair of her pubis. "Show me, Psyche. I want to know."

"Mistress, please, put down your dress."

The Queen of the Dead dropped her gown, silver tears filling her eyes. Psyche had feared angering her, but she had shamed the goddess instead. A wave of melancholy surged over the chamber. The dark corners seemed to grow darker. Where another goddess would have grown angry, Proserpina became quiet. A great sadness descended on Psyche. Without warning, a feeling of isolation overtook her, and she too began to cry.

Until this moment, Psyche had thought she had been a powerless victim of loneliness. In her husband's palace, she had yearned for human companionship, but every night he had come and given her love. Even in her travails, Venus had offered her choices. If she had abandoned her quest to see her husband again, her beauty and fame would have served her well enough. She could have been taken care of for the rest of her life by anyone she chose.

Yet Proserpina had been abducted by the coldest god of all. Shuddering, Psyche remembered that it was her husband's fault. He had shot Pluto with a golden arrow as the daughter of Ceres gathered flowers. Yet the God of Love had not thought to shoot the maiden as well.

When King Jupiter had forced the marriage, Ceres had wept for her daughter and punished the earth, but she could not have her back. Unlike Psyche, Proserpina could not stop her torment. Indeed, she had no choices. Even when she was above ground in the spring and summer, she was condemned to return to this dark silent place to feed the need of a cruel husband for all eternity.

"Goddess," Psyche said, touching the hem of her gown, "please, don't cry. I would be honored to show you what love feels like. It is just that it must be done in the right way. A little more slowly." Psyche glanced toward the inner chamber.

"Come then," Proserpina said, standing. Psyche followed. The dark bedroom was also lit with the lamps of trapped souls, though they seemed to burn brighter here. The bed frame was a large amethyst shaped like an open palm. Black silk cushions covered the jagged purple crystal. On the goddess's bedside table was a mirror framed in diamonds and brushes and bottles of pure gold. Jewelry was piled high, each piece priceless. Earrings of diamonds glittered in the light, necklaces of gold and silver shone brightly, rings and bracelets crafted by the finest work-men. Yet none of these things gave the goddess pleasure.

The Queen of the Underworld sat on her bed and grasped Psyche's hand to pull her on to the bed. Psyche resisted.

Would the goddess's bed be considered her seat? Surely that meant her throne—but if there was any possible way to trap her here, Psyche did not doubt the queen would do it.

"Mistress…"

"Call me Proserpina. I tire of being called only mistress by mortals. I am more than wife, daughter, or queen. Speak my name, Psyche. You came here to seek me out, and you have found me."

"Proserpina," she said, trembling to hear a name synonymous with destruction escape her lips.

"Go on, tell me. No, show me. I want you to touch me, the way your husband touched you."

Psyche went behind Proserpina and gathered her thick black hair in her hands, revealing a necklace of bruises that encircled her pale throat. Psyche had similar marks on her own neck, but they were from her enemy, not her husband.

"Proserpina," she whispered in the goddess's ear, touching the lobe with her lips, "I will teach you about desire."

"Proserpina." She forced herself to whisper the name again, as if casting her own spell. "You have been bent to the will of those more powerful than you, but now it is time to take your own pleasure. I will gladly share with you the gift my husband gave me."

The goddess's shoulders relaxed as Psyche sucked her earlobe.

After trailing her tongue down Proserpina's neck, she tenderly kissed the bruises, inhaling the goddess's scent of deep earth and dried flowers.

Following her instinct, Psyche stroked the goddess's breasts through the fabric of her dress sharp with diamonds. She teased Proserpina's nipples, one then the other, until they grew hard and the goddess closed her eyes. Psyche placed her hand above the collar line and plunged her hand into Proserpina's gown.

The goddess's breasts were firm and high, smaller than Psyche's own. As though by instinct, Proserpina jerked away.

"I did not mean to," the goddess said softly. "I want you to. It is just…"

But Psyche understood. "Do not think of him, Proserpina. Give yourself to me. I will teach you truly what it is to be woman. There is pleasure in your body just waiting to be explored. Yield to my hands now."

Heeding her words, the Queen of the Dead acquiesced, giving herself over to Psyche's caress. Soon the goddess moaned softly and squirmed, eager for more.

"Now, Mistress, you can lift your skirts."

Proserpina lifted her gown quickly. Her legs were shapely, but too thin. No matter how old she was, she would always appear to be a maiden. But, Psyche decided, on this day, the Queen of the Underworld would at long last know what pleasure was.

The goddess lay back on the bed and parted her thighs. Psyche came around to the front. Though Psyche had been in this state herself, she had never seen another in it or examined a woman's sex. The glittering black hair was that of a goddess but the pale pink flesh beneath was the same as a mortal's. The dark goddess lay before Psyche—her legs spread, her eyes closed, hungering for a lover's touch. Psyche was glad to be the one to give it to her.

Moving her fingers along the skin of the goddess's inner thigh, Psyche teased her until Proserpina moaned and tipped her pelvis in anticipation. Psyche fingered the goddess's pink bud, enjoying the sensation of how wet she had already made her.

She wanted suddenly to fill Proserpina, to make her writhe and beg for more. Smiling, she rubbed Proserpina's bud back and forth more and more quickly until the goddess jerked against Psyche's fingers, hardening with desire. Psyche imagined using her tongue the way her husband had. She could picture herself climbing on the giant amethyst bed, with her head between the goddess's thighs, making the Queen of the Dead open herself wider and wider until Psyche had her completely at her mercy. But she stared at the light of the souls intertwined for eternity and stopped her hands from casting their magic.

"Mistress—Proserpina, forgive me. I will gladly give you what you ask, but I beg you, promise not to trap me here. Promise to give me what I have come for and allow me to return to the light of day, alive with a chance to see my husband again."

Proserpina's eyes flashed open. Psyche was unprepared for the rage she found there. Proserpina glanced down at her glittering pubis and Psyche's retreated hand.

"Clever girl. How I would like to keep you as my handmaiden, a warm companion by my side for the rest of your days." She gazed at Psyche's belly, hidden beneath her dusky-rose *stola*. "And your little godling, what joy she would bring to these dark halls."

Proserpina sat up suddenly and Psyche inadvertently took a step back. The goddess grinned at her fear, reached forward, and pulled Psyche to her. She caressed Psyche's cheek and ran her forefinger to her temple, sending an image of Psyche and Proserpina holding a baby, a golden light filling the shadowed halls, a smile on the goddess's lips.

"Stay with me, Psyche. It will be a better fate for you than doing Venus's bidding. I will be a good companion to you."

But as Proserpina kept her finger on Psyche's temple, the image behind her eyes changed. It seemed that the dark halls grew even darker as they both saw the deep sorrow that filled

Psyche. Without her love, she was lost. The baby's happy coos turned to cries ringing out through the empty halls.

"Little mother, Venus sent you here to be mine or my husband's. You would be much safer with me." But the image of the possible future revealed Psyche on her knees weeping bitter tears, holding her child close and begging to be released.

The goddess sighed. "Ah, well, having been kept against my will, I suppose I could not do that to another, even a mortal. Very well, I promise that in exchange for pleasure, I will give you what you have come for. I will allow you to return to the land of the living, but you must please me well."

"I will, Mistress—Proserpina. I cannot stay with you, but I will give you a gift, so you can feel this once I'm gone." Psyche put her hands on the goddess, pushing her back down onto the soft cushions of her bed and knelt next to the bed.

"Pull down your gown, Mistress."

Proserpina did not hesitate to expose her breasts, small and pert like a maiden. Her skin was white as marble. Psyche lowered her head, a strand of her golden hair escaped, brushing the goddess's breast. Using her tongue, Psyche began to lick Proserpina's areolas until her nipples hardened.

The goddess held her body taut in anticipation as Psyche took her nipple between her lips sucking gently at first and then harder until Proserpina gasped and thrust her breast into Psyche's mouth. Only then did Psyche return her hand to the goddess's mound, teasing the outer lips gently with her fingers, making the goddess move to her. She released her nipple and began to stroke the goddess's bud again. Proserpina gasped in pleasure and Psyche smiled at the revelation on her face.

"Touch your breast," Psyche said. "For you to have pleasure, goddess, you must own your body." The Queen of the Underworld did as she was bid, taking her wet nipple between her fingers and rubbing it gently.

"Now, take your other hand and place it atop mine."

Feeling the warmth of the goddess's palm against the back her own hand and the wetness of the goddess's desire, Psyche was eager for Proserpina to finally understand.

But, suddenly, Psyche felt the same cold emptiness that had permeated the throne room. An unseen presence watched. Wild-eyed, she gazed around but saw nothing. Yet the place it emanated from was clear to her though nothing could be seen with the naked eye.

She imagined what the Lord of the Dead saw from under his helm of invisibility—Psyche, golden-haired, colored by the sun, kneeling next to pale, dark-haired Proserpina, her mortal hand buried in the goddess's dark mound, with the goddess's pale, elegant hand atop. Psyche's heart beat in fear. Were her actions arousing the King of the Underworld, angering him or both? Proserpina did not seem to notice any change and she urged Psyche on by pushing against her. They could not stop now. She stroked Proserpina's silken bud and the goddess moaned, spreading her legs wider, silently begging for release.

No, Psyche decided, not even the King of the Underworld could prevent his wife from this.

Moving her finger slightly, Psyche drew closer and whispered, "Proserpina, touch yourself. Make your own pleasure." She let out her warm mortal breath, gently nipping the goddess's ear, as she slid her own hand away.

Proserpina smiled as if she had waited all of eternity to be told this. She closed her eyes, working her fingers quickly over her bud while rolling her nipple in her other hand. It was a wondrous sight, but Psyche was ill at ease, knowing that Pluto watched.

As the goddess climaxed, she transformed from a pale, dark-haired maiden to a vibrant honey-haired girl, kissed by the sun and ready to frolic with nymphs. The change was only there for a moment. When Psyche looked again, the dark-haired queen lay on her bed, a small smile on her lips.

When Proserpina opened her eyes, they seemed a shade lighter as if pleasing herself had let a little sun into her immortal soul. "I see now." The Queen of the Dead breathed. "If my husband could, if he only wanted to do that…" A silver tear trailed her cheek.

"Don't," Psyche said. Looking to where he had stood, but when she felt for him in her mind, there was nothing. He was gone.

"Don't think of him. Proserpina, this is for you. Here." She placed the flat of her hand against the goddess's glittering vulva. The goddess spasmed with the pleasure of her touch, writhing against Psyche's palm. "Sometimes," Psyche whispered, "it can happen again."

The goddess's eyes grew wide in surprise. She breathed deeply, contemplating all she had learned. She righted her dress and sat up. Color had come into her cheeks and though she did not look happy, she appeared less miserable.

"You have given me a gift, Psyche, and I will give you one in return." She cupped her hands together and opened them to reveal a small, black wooden box. "I will give you what you have come for, the box Venus desires you bring her. Listen to me now, do not open it. What is inside is only fit for a goddess. It is too much for a mortal. Do you understand?"

"Yes, Mistress."

"I hope so. You are a mortal unlike any other, but I fear your curiosity will be your undoing. Oh, little mother, how I long to keep you, for your own protection as well as my own need. Go now, quickly."

Psyche bowed her head. "Thank you, Mistress." She wanted to say more. A part of her longed to stay with the goddess, just for a little while, but there was no little while in the Underworld. She turned and walked out of the inner sanctum and down the stairs to the main part of the palace.

CHAPTER 12

BY THE RIVER STYX

Psyche stood straight and held her head high, but inside she quaked with fear. The King of the Dead would never allow her to leave Hades. She did not know where he would catch her, only that he would.

After leaving the palace, she found her way to the entrance guarded by Cerberus and threw him the second barley cake. He ran after it, all three heads snapping and growling at each other. But even after getting free of the monstrous dog, she could hardly breathe, waiting for Pluto to overtake her.

Along the banks of the River Styx, shades fluttered about, unknowing, lost. This dark and somber place was where she had wanted to come to relieve her own misery. When her husband had forbidden her from taking her life, she had thought him cruel. Yet there would always be enough time for this. Even if Pluto permitted her to leave, she would be back. There was no other option.

And then she felt him—a cold sense of permanence. She turned, but he was shrouded in his helm of invisibility. Fearing further angering him, she did not dare address him. Instead, she stopped and stared at the place the emptiness emanated from. He did not reveal himself. She continued on her way, resisting the urge to run.

The dock was crowded. Shades lingered there, unsure of where to go. If they were not heroes, villains, or initiated into the mysteries, it really did not matter. They could drink from the River Lethe, the Fountain of Memory, or just drift.

Charon poled his boat crowded with the shades of the newly buried toward the dock. Psyche decided to wait no longer. Turning to the empty space where Pluto stood, she knelt before him.

"All-Seeing King, I beg your leave to return above ground where I belong."

He removed his helm, his cruel lips in a snarl that might have been a grin.

"How did you know I was here?"

"I, I just knew. The first time and..." Psyche stopped herself. It was better not to admit she had sensed him in Proserpina's bedchamber.

Pluto stroked his beard, as if contemplating a tasty morsel he would soon pluck from his platter.

"Give me one reason why I should permit you to return to the land of the living."

"The Goddess of Love and Beauty sent me here to retrieve this box from the queen—and to return with it."

"I don't think Venus really expects you to come back. I've asked her to send me a concubine—and you will do nicely." His eyes were half-cocked, as if he were already savoring her flesh.

"My husband is the God of Love."

"Is he now? What god sends his wife to Hades? It appears he is done with you, little Psyche."

"No, he loves me still."

"How do you know?" He asked, echoing the question that tormented her constantly.

"This," she said showing him her wedding band, a snake

eating its own tail. "If he no longer loved me, this would have fallen off, but as it is, it won't come off, and..." She stopped herself too late.

He raised his bushy eyebrows. "How else? Has he marked you as his own? Prove it to me and I'll let you go."

Psyche frantically tried to think of a way out, but there was nothing else to be done.

"Please, All-seeing King, swear you'll let me go if I show you."

"I swear," he said glancing at the River Styx.

Not wanting to turn her back to him, Psyche turned to the side. She began to raise her gown, trying to do it as modestly as possible. His eyes grew wide in anticipation. At the sight of her naked thigh, he licked his lips. She lifted her gown to reveal her left buttock and glanced down to make sure the mark was still there.

The moment her eyes were off him he was upon her. He grabbed her roughly, capturing her hands and holding them with one of his.

"No!" she screamed, struggling, weightless against his strength. "No! You swore!"

He lifted her gown and pushed her over so she was folded before him completely exposed. As he began lifting his own robe, she struggled against him, but it was like fighting a mountain. Looking behind her, she saw his hardened shaft, huge and dark with blood.

"My husband will come!" she screamed. "I belong to the God of Love!"

Laughing, he pushed her legs apart with his own.

"He will punish you for this! If you do this, he will have vengeance!"

But the King of the Underworld ignored her words. Her screams echoed across the river. A few shades turned in her direction, but there was no sound other than her voice and his laughter.

His cold hands were on her skin, hungry for her living flesh. He gripped her haunches roughly. The child in her womb would not survive this. Pluto's seed would be like lava, searing anything alive. She tried to fight, to fall away from him, to slink out of his embrace. She bucked against him, thrashing with all her might, but he held her tight.

"Ah, how I've missed a woman who fights. How very kind of Venus to send you to me."

Psyche attempted once more to pull away, feeling his shaft against her thigh.

"No!" she screamed, knowing it would do her no good.

His hand moved to her buttocks close to the place her husband had marked her. She jerked away and when he touched her again, his hand was directly on the mark.

Hissing suddenly in protest, he withdrew, loosening his grip on her hands. Her husband's mark had burned him! Psyche disentangled herself from him and turned. When he reached for her again, she held up her left wrist so he grabbed her bracelet. He growled as it too burned him. Perplexed, Pluto held up his reddened palm, his brow furrowing in confusion. He did not seem terribly hurt or angry, but the shock had stolen his lust.

He dropped his robes which again lay flat across his waist. Touching her where she was marked had made him flaccid.

Her own clothes covering her again, she scrambled away. Trembling violently, she feared she might swoon, but she could not risk fainting.

"You swore" she said, gasping for breath, "by the River Styx."

He raised an eyebrow. "I did not say, 'by the River Styx.' I was merely standing by the River Styx. Besides, I did not swear to let you go unscathed." He eyed her warily, cradling his burned hand with the other. "Go now, strange creature. You will return to me soon enough. And I will remember. I will have plans for you, little Psyche. You will warm my bed while my queen is above ground—there are ways to make a shade have form. And I will have you for eternity. I will make you drink from the Fountain of Memory, so you remember what you have lost and what each night will bring. Do not think you have escaped me, for no mortal escapes the King of the Dead." His steely eyes ate at her for a moment before he put on his helm and vanished.

When he was gone, she fell to her knees trembling in the dust of Hades, too ill to stand. She told herself to rise and go quickly from this place, yet it took all her will just to get up.

The next time Charon poled his ferry to the dock, she was waiting. As the shades disembarked, she searched her pouch. Her hand shook too badly at first to find the coin. Had she lost it? Charon would not wait for her, nor would he let her on the ferry without payment. Plunging her hand into her pouch, she searched frantically—barley cake, water, Proserpina's box, and at last the *denarii*. She held it out to him, but he refused it. With a trembling hand, she put it in her mouth and only then did he reach to take it from her, finally allowing her to board.

Her heart calmed as the boat moved away from Hades and back to the land of the living. It would do no good to think of what had almost happened. She feared that cramps would come, that she would leave the baby here in the Land of the Dead.

Psyche held on to the brief image Proserpina had shown her of the two of them holding the baby. Her daughter, golden-eyed like her father, with a sweet rosebud mouth, and wings, little white baby-wings. This child would be powerful. She would not allow her mother's fear to dislodge her from her womb. She would hold fast and grow into a demigoddess.

When Charon docked the boat, Psyche stepped off quickly before the shades could board. She moved away from the river, determined to make as much distance from herself and Hades as possible.

As she scrambled up the hill, she tried to convince herself it was all behind her. Pluto had not had her, but the dread of his final words weighed on her heart. There would be no escape from him. She could not think of him now. Instead, her thoughts turned to her husband. At least she would have the chance to tell him before she died. That was what mattered, and with luck her baby would be born. If the gods willed it, she would not die giving birth.

Seeing the sunlight up ahead, her heart began to lift. She had gone to the Underworld and returned! Only Odysseus, Hercules, Theseus, Orpheus, and Aeneas had done this. Three of them demigods. Heroes all, except Orpheus. And she, who was only a woman, had done it, too! Her heart swelled with pride. Only a woman who had bested the Goddess of Love and Beauty!

She laughed softly to herself, savoring a moment of triumph. She had met all of Venus's trials and succeeded where the goddess expected her to fail. The golden light of day shone just outside the cavern. Was this the place where Orpheus had turned around and lost Eurydice again? Psyche would not make his mistake.

At last, she reentered the land of the living. The sun immediately brought back color, light, and warmth. She examined her hands in the sunlight, thinking of all they had done. Underneath the dust of Hades, were her hands still lovely? Would people still think her the second coming of Venus? No, her hands looked old. The doubt Care's whip had sown in her heart returned. Her trials had aged her and the pregnancy, too, though it hardly showed yet, would distort her body. Venus had been right when she had taunted Psyche; as a mortal, her beauty was fleeting.

Her husband had said it was her soul, not her physical beauty that he loved, but she wondered. What if he found her displeasing to the eye? Having always taken her appearance for granted, she had never worked on it as others did. Now she regretted it. If her face looked as dried out and haggard as her hands... If her husband saw her, would he question why he had ever found her beautiful?

Noticing that her hair had come out of her braid, she

attempted to fix it and saw how ashen and dull it had become, as if the colorless world of Hades had robbed her of the golden color.

Reaching into her pouch, she brought out the bladder of water. After drinking some, she tried to wash her face, but it was not enough. What she needed was a proper beauty treatment, a bath, creams, and makeup. Yet Venus was unlikely to allow her any of these things before permitting her to see her husband. As she put the bladder back into the pouch, she felt the box of Proserpina's beauty. Yes! If Venus could use some then so could Psyche—just use a tiny amount. Remembering but not heeding Proserpina's warning, she took the box out and held it in her hand. It seemed too small to be powerful, and besides, Psyche had done what no other mortal woman could, surely a drop of the goddess's beauty would not undo her.

Gingerly lifting the lid, she peeked inside. A dark shadow slid into the light, blocking out the sunlight above her. Psyche gasped, trying to close the box too late as the shadow swarmed out and enveloped her. Regret engulfed her as she realized she had fallen into the goddess's trap after all. The last sound she heard was Venus's victorious laughter.

Psyche's body fell to the ground and there she stayed. Her spirit drifted above, seeing what was not clear to the naked eye. Morpheus, God of Sleep, blue and serene, stood guard on one side of her unconscious body. Though she had never seen him, he was familiar from all the nights he had held her in his embrace. His huge black wings spread wide, sheltering her body and her spirit. At first she did not understand why, but then she saw two figures in the cavern to Hades. One of the shadows stood large, grinning wide. It was Pluto, licking his pale pink lips. His hands reached out toward her body, his fingers itching to touch her.

"So soon, little Psyche, I had not expected it to be so soon. I will have you while you're still warm."

The other figure was obscure, indistinct, but obviously one of

Pluto's slaves. The form was black as tar and as all consuming. It lurched forward toward her body, but Morpheus brushed it back with a wing. It was Thanatos. Death was waiting to take her back from whence she had just come.

Unable to move or respond, she could only lie there, hating herself. Her husband and Proserpina had warned her that curiosity would be her undoing. Now she would never see her love again. She would have wept, would have screamed and torn her hair, but her body was immobile and her spirit could only watch.

"Give her to me, Morpheus," Pluto said. "She is mine now."

"No," the God of Sleep responded. His voice was lazy and soft, like velvet, like moss. Just hearing the slight melody of his speech made her spirit drowsy. Though he did not touch her body, it was as if he cradled her gently, a soft layer of protection from the King of the Dead. "She is not yours yet, King of Shadows."

"But she will be," the other snapped. "All mortals are mine eventually."

"Perhaps."

"You have no claim on this one, Morpheus."

"No, King of Shadows. She is not yet dead, merely asleep. And while she lives, another claims her as his own."

Thanatos made another move toward her, but Morpheus brushed him off with his wing.

Suddenly a loud crack echoed through the sky. Psyche saw rather than felt a great wind blow over the trees near the cavern, and in a flash of movement, the God of Love flew down to her body.

His wings glistened in the sun, his muscles shone with oil. Even in spirit form, Psyche could feel the power emanating from him. Unable to call out, she could only watch as he glared at Thanatos, who seemed to disappear.

"Wise men keep their wives locked inside the house, Shooter," Pluto said, smirking. Though he stayed hidden in the cavern, the

King of the Dead's crown glittered with light and his voice seemed to come from the rock itself. But her husband, quick and agile, had no fear of Pluto as he fluttered between Morpheus and the mouth of Hades.

"That is good counsel, King of the Dead. When your wife rises to the surface come spring, I'll be sure to keep an eye on her. In fact, perhaps my wife and I will ensure she has a delightful time on Olympus away from your gloomy realm."

Pluto's eyes began to burn like hot coals. He took a step toward the winged one, but hesitated as the God of Love drew his bow.

"Enjoy your mortal while you have her, Shooter. In the end, she will belong to me, and she will pay for your crimes."

The God of Love took quick aim and shot into the cavern, but his arrow did not find its mark. The King of the Underworld had vanished.

Staring at Psyche's unconscious body, the God of Love spoke to the other immortal.

"Morpheus, I owe you a debt of gratitude for not allowing that vile creature to have her. Whatever you need, I will gladly give you."

"I am merely doing my job. Your mortal is trapped between sleep and death. I simply did not allow Thanatos to tip the scales." Morpheus lowered his black wings so the God of Love could lift his wife's body in his strong arms and hold her close to his heart.

"My soul, what have I done?" Silver tears flowed from his eyes, but he did not bother to wipe them away. Shifting her weight to one arm, he lifted his hand and swept the shadow from her as if cleaning cobwebs from an old pot. His hand caressed her face, moving down to her breasts, belly, pubis, and thighs. Light as a feather, he stroked her ankles and feet, dusting the shadow of death-sleep from her until he wound it in his hand and held it away from her.

He gazed at the box and it floated to his waiting hand.

"Return to your rightful place and trouble this woman no more," he commanded. The shadow streamed back into the box and vanished, and with it Morpheus disappeared.

"Forgive me, Psyche. Come back to me, my soul." He stroked her neck tenderly, kissing the bruises and making them disappear.

Suddenly she was no longer staring down at her body from above. Her spirit was pulled back in. She opened her eyes and looked into his golden ones.

"Husband." She could say no more as emotions flooded her.

Finally he had come for her. As she relaxed into his arms, the terror of all her trials overcame her. The other immortals had tormented her, yet they were of no consequence to him. Pluto had almost raped her, but had vanished once her husband raised his bow.

A sudden fury assailed her, the heat of her anger as strong as love. Where had he been? Why had he made her suffer so? An urge to slap the face she had longed to see overtook her. The thought shocked her. How surprised he would be if she rejected him! She almost laughed aloud.

Her love for him was fierce, more determined than she had ever imagined. And yet he, a god, had been recovering from a minor burn while she toiled for a simple chance to speak to him one last time.

Perhaps she should take Venus's advice and find a mortal husband. Or better yet, be done with love completely—take the blue butterfly wings and fly into the sky. She pictured herself, more heavily pregnant, naked and flying with her own wings, beholden to no man. She would stop in cities and bless supplicants, become a goddess after all. In spring and summer, she could visit Proserpina and Ceres. The goddesses would gladly help her with the baby. In the fall, she could live with Pan, his goats giving the baby milk. In the winter, she could go back to her father's palace. But even imagining this fantasy, she knew her heart would ache for her husband. The baby's golden eyes would be a painful reminder. Even in anger and despite all her suffering, Psyche loved him still.

Before she could decide on her response, he spoke.

"Forgive me, my soul, my mother locked me in her palace and despite all my efforts, I could not escape. She claimed that the burn you caused was a great wound, but it was nothing compared to the pain of being without you.

"All this time, I have been like a physician who has never been ill. I thought love was a game. I had wanted to punish you with a broken heart, but instead I discovered heartache myself. You must know that I never wanted any of these things to happen to you. I've been sick with fear for you. Finally, I shot my way out of my mother's place. I swear by the River Styx, I will never allow you to be in danger again."

She glanced toward the cavern that led to the Underworld. Pluto was right, all mortals would be his eventually.

"No," he said as if reading her thoughts. "You will never belong to him! I will take you to Olympus and demand that King Jupiter make you an immortal."

She did not respond immediately, imagining him locked away while she toiled.

"Did he hurt you?" He asked, anguish in his voice. His tears flowed more freely, like mercury sliding down his cheeks. He held his hand over her pubis, seeming to sense she had not been violated. "Can you forgive me, Psyche?" His beautiful face in torment was more than she could bear.

"Yes, husband. I am relieved that you did not watch my torment with approval."

"No, Psyche, quite the opposite. I did everything in my power to escape, to get the other gods to help you. But you, my love, made an equal rival for my mother. Never has she been more threatened by a mortal woman. Why did you persist so?"

Psyche laughed, her voice slightly raw. Why, indeed? She wondered now that it was all over.

"I could not let you go, husband. I did not believe you no longer loved me. And I, I wanted to tell you the reason I disobeyed you."

"I know it was your sisters."

"No. It's true that they encouraged me to light the lamp and to get a knife. I wouldn't have thought of those things myself. But in the end, I lit the lamp because I was in love with you, the winged one, the God of Love, but I also loved you, my shadow husband, and I could not stand the thought that I was being unfaithful to you in my heart. I had to know that it was you, that I loved you for who you were in the day and at night."

"But how could you love me like that? I never shot you with my arrows."

"No, you didn't need to. I only needed to look into your eyes that once, to talk to you and feel your hands on me in the night. It was a new kind of love. One that grew between us naturally."

He stared at her a moment, as if she were an odd creature, the kind of which he had never encountered before. But his gaze softened and he pulled her to him and kissed her. She kissed him back, his tongue sliding into her mouth. She sucked on it as he stood, lifting her. He spread his wings wide and she relaxed into his embrace.

As he flew straight up into the clouds, he shifted her in his arms so she was tight against him as she had been the first time. He plunged his hand into her gown, ripping the fabric a little as he brought out her breast. She clung to him with her thighs, pulling her dress over her hips. Her mound rubbed against his abdomen as it had before. His hand slipped to her buttocks, holding her where he had marked her. Vibrations of pleasure coursed through her. This was where his hand belonged.

She kissed his lips fervently as he flew over land, over palaces and pastures, temples and orchards. He broke off their kiss to take her breast into his mouth, flicking his tongue over her nipple. She breathed in the scent of his hair, ambrosia, sun, and feathers.

Putting his hand on his breechcloth, he pulled himself free. His hardness against her skin made her moan in anticipation. She had grown wet against his belly as she had the first time, and he lifted her ever so slightly and slid inside her.

Amidst her pleasure, she opened her eyes to the brightness of the sun. Beneath them were fields and houses. Anyone could see them among the clouds, but she did not care. She had longed to be able to see him all this time and now, shining in the sun amid the slowly darkening sky, watching him was its own pleasure.

But something nagged at her. Though they were thoroughly entwined, she could not give herself to him the way she wanted.

"Husband."

He released her nipple to look into her eyes.

"How will you get King Jupiter to agree? What if he refuses?"

But her husband laughed, gripping her buttocks and lifting her then thrusting into her in a way that made it hard to focus on any worry.

"Oh, my soul, do you not remember?" He pushed into her again, making her moan and cling to him even more tightly. "I am a monster, feared by gods and men. The other immortals will do as I wish or they will suffer." He thrust into her once more so she was consumed by desire. She laughed softly as she surrendered herself to him completely, and they rocked together as they flew over the land and up to the heavens.

AFTERWORD

The Romans believed that love was, in fact, a monster. To fall in love and lose control of rational thought was a horror to them. This, along with the idea of a secret husband who comes to a lonely woman at night, was part of what compelled me to write *Psyche Unbound*. To me, Cupid and Psyche has elements of Beauty and the Beast, with a dash of Rumpelstiltskin. All of this laid the groundwork for an exciting adventure.

The myth of Cupid and Psyche was first recorded as a story within a story in *The Golden Ass or Metamorphoses* by Apuleius in the 2nd century CE. Although I loosely followed the original myth, I changed a few significant details. For example, Psyche is originally led to a mountain top in a funeral-like procession to be married. I also excluded an additional task Venus gives her and of course added and made up many details.

It's notable that Psyche is the only woman to go and return from Hades on her own. There are many Greco-Roman myths that involve a journey and a series of trials, but very few have heroines, and even less have heroines who survive and live happily ever after—especially after angering a goddess. In the original story, Psyche does indeed drink ambrosia and become immortal. She and Cupid have a daughter whom they name Pleasure. Venus, fickle in all things, accepts Jupiter's decision and even dances at the wedding.

Like Apuleius's original tale, *Psyche Unbound* had many metamorphoses of its own. I'm so grateful to early readers Joann Lo, Darienne Heatherman, Elise Tissot, Carrie Quinn, Ariel Senseman, Michelle Lang, Kevin Awakuni, and especially Planaria Price and Diane Pershing for help on early drafts. Special thanks to Meghan Farrell, Danielle Rayner, Lindsey Stover and everyone at Tule Publishing. A big thank you to the Los Angeles Romance Authors where I've met so many wonderful writers. I'm also grateful to my husband for giving me time and support to write. And special thanks to television. Without TV occupying my children on weekend mornings, I would not have been able to write *Psyche Unbound*. Thank you, Dinosaur Train! And thank you, dear reader, for reading all the way to the end!

THE QUEEN OF WARRIORS

Ephesus, Winter, 244 BCE

Alexandra knelt before the priestess in the darkened cavern amid the flickering lamps. She had been to every temple from Isfahan to Ephesus and sacrificed to no avail, but she had never expected to find herself here.

"What do you want from the goddess?" the priestess asked, eyeing her with distrust.

Alexandra was fairly sure the priestess knew who she was—who she had been—but she did not think the old woman would turn her in for the price on her head.

"I wish to break the curse that haunts me." She spoke from low in her throat, an intimacy between the two of them. This was the secret she had longed to say aloud for the last three years, and here it was. She stopped herself from saying what else she longed for—to find any of her men who still lived, especially Aristos and Nicandor, and ask for forgiveness before she died.

The priestess's one blind eye and one seeing eye passed over Alexandra's muscles and scars. The old bitch had made her strip for this ritual, and now she stared, her eyes lingering over Alexandra's golden necklaces, bracelets, and rings.

"The goddess cannot break the curse," the priestess said. "But if you wish, I will ask Hecate to open the gate. Then you may speak to the one who cursed you. Then you can beg for forgiveness."

Alexandra was not one to beg. She did not fear living men. But Hecate, the triple-headed goddess, the keeper of the cross-roads, the goddess of witches—Hecate—the name was like an ice-cold blade on her naked flesh.

Yet Alexandra had traversed all the way from deep within the heart of Asia Minor to come here to Ephesus. She had expected the great temple of Artemis to be her destination, but she had been summoned to this cave shrine of Hecate.

She would see it through. "I seek only one of the dead. Will others cross the gate?"

The priestess grinned, exposing her broken teeth. "That depends on your crimes, warrior woman. If those you killed lay unburied and haunt the land of the living, longing for vengeance, they may come through as well."

"Can they harm me?"

"They are merely shades. It is for you to account for the lives you've taken."

Alexandra lifted her chin. "I regret not a single one of the men I killed, only the deaths I failed to prevent. For those I repent, and for those I am willing to pay, with my life if need be."

"It will not be that easy." The priestess withdrew a dagger from a sheath on her waist. The sacrificial blade was short and dark, bronze instead of steel, and had been forged long ago. "Your people know the goddess yearns for mortal blood, as do the shades of the dead. Take this and give them what you will." She handed Alexandra the dagger, hilt first. "Though I can see you are shrouded in sorrow, it is not your time to die yet. Don't cut too deep."

Alexandra approached the black goddess stone on her knees. She raised her left arm, whispered a name, and cut her wrist so the blood began to flow.

The priestess drew a circle around Alexandra and the stone. She pulled a pouch from her robes, uttered an incantation, and sprinkled an herb over the lamps. Soon the scent of myrrh and honey mixed with the iron smell of Alexandra's blood filled the cavern.

Once the gate to the Underworld opened, the priestess left. Shades of fallen warriors filled the sanctuary, shouting oaths no louder than the wind. Alexandra stared at them, trying to find a familiar face. Though she had lost enough blood to swoon, she swayed on her knees, her back straight, and spoke loudly to the shades.

"If I killed you in battle, you died honorably. If it shames you to have been killed by a woman, know I am not any woman. I am of Sparta—any of my countrymen would have dispatched you just as quickly. Go from this place now, drink from the River Lethe, and find peace."

The shades did not leave, but they quieted. Her skin prickled with gooseflesh. It was not only fear. Despite the smoke and flames, the temple had grown cold.

One shadow who had been silent all along now grew strong on her blood. Though still transparent and dark, it gained form.

Suddenly able to see the shade, tears came to her eyes.

"Beloved," she said, her voice breaking, "forgive me. I did not mean it to happen. Tell me what to do. I will give you my life if you wish it."

The shade gazed at her with a mixture of love, bitterness, and vengeance.

Vishanti, the shade said, the sound no more than a whisper. *I cursed you in love, and only by love or justice can you break the curse. You must right the wrongs you have done and face your deepest fear. Return to Rhagae and pay for your crimes.*

Alexandra swayed on her knees and brought her hands to her face, allowing herself to sob only once. She had planned to return to Sparta. After all this time, she had been about to journey across the sea, to finally go home. But it seemed the gods had other plans for her.

CHAPTER ONE: ARTAXERXES'S PRIZE

Rhagae, Spring 243 BCE

"You must go," Alexandra said to the noseless man. She had released her slaves and those who followed her in Ephesus, but the noseless man and her Persian handmaiden, Dari, had insisted on accompanying her to Rhagae.

"No, little queen. I have lived with you and fought with you. If the gods will it, I will die with you."

"Horses," Dari said. "They found us."

Ten Persian chargers galloped toward them. The sun glinted off their breastplates and shields painted with golden lynxes.

Alexandra and the noseless man drew their swords as the riders surrounded them.

"Are you the Queen of Warriors?" a Persian archer asked in common Greek.

This made her laugh. As if any other Greek woman would wear a leather dress and breastplate under her cloak. As if any other Greek woman would stand in Rhagae and hold a sword.

"What do you think?" she asked, staring up at him. Standing back-to-back with the noseless man, they turned in a circle, pointing their swords. "Who among you will be my last kill?"

The archer could have shot her then. But he didn't. There must still be a price on her head if she was taken alive. Four riders dismounted.

Let me die to the sound of sword song, she thought as she ran at one of the Persians. He dropped his shield, and she beat him back, waiting to be struck from behind. Instead her opponent succeeded in slicing her left bicep.

"Don't kill her!" a Persian shouted in Aramaic. A rider came from behind and threw a net over her. She struggled to free herself but was knocked to the ground. Still grasping her sword, she scrambled to rise, but a man gripped her shoulders hard, squeezing her cut bicep.

"Drop the sword."

"No." She would die with it in her hand. But when they stepped on her wrist, she relented. She scanned the ground for the noseless man and Dari but saw nothing but horse hoofs.

After she was disarmed, her wrists were bound. They blindfolded her and forced her up onto one of the horses, in front of a rider who gripped her tightly.

"Artaxerxes will take care of you," the Persian said in common Greek. "Soon enough, we'll see your head on our gates."

Artaxerxes had taken Rhagae two years earlier, killing the Greek satrap she had helped put in power, but what worried her more was that Artaxerxes had once fought for Red Wind, the man who had been her undoing and put the price on her head.

"What have I done?" Alexandra asked lightly.

"Do you deny being the Queen of Warriors?" the Persian asked.

"Once, long ago. But no more."

"No," the Persian growled in her ear. "No more." The horse slowed, and he dismounted, pulling her down roughly. She stumbled but did not fall. On the wind, she heard word being relayed that she had been caught alive. They were keeping her here so the people could assemble.

The jubilation of the crowd could be heard from a distance. Shouts and laughter, as if it were a festival day and she the main entertainment. A long rope was wrapped around her bound wrists and given to another horse rider. She feared being dragged for a moment, but then she remembered the price on her head.

This was a processional; everyone wanted to see her alive before her execution.

Focusing on her steps, she listened to the movement of those around her. There were perhaps ten men whose job it was to guard her, to keep her from escaping, and to prevent the crowd from killing her.

"Hail Artaxerxes, the Golden Lynx of Rhagae!"

It must be this Artaxerxes who held the other end of the rope, leading her into the city as his prize.

As she walked, she shook out her hair, loosening the blindfold. Through a sliver of vision, she followed the rope to Artaxerxes, who sat astride a bay stallion. The sun shone off his silver Greek helmet. Long black hair cascaded down his back, loosely bound in a braid. In typical Persian style, he wore leather trousers and had a bow slung across his back—if only she could get it, this would all be over quickly.

"Murderer!" a man in the crowd shouted.

Another laughed. "The Terror of the East no more!"

"Ahura Mazda has heard my prayers. The Queen of Warriors will die in Rhagae," a third cried.

It was true she had once been known as the Terror of the East, a Greek woman fighting for a Greek king to keep his Persian subjects loyal. Her advisor, Nicandor the Little Red Fox, had sent out rumors she was merciless and fierce, holding no weakness in her heart, for she loved no man. Though many had tried to win her love, none had succeeded, losing their lives and armies to her instead.

"Death to the Queen of Warriors!"

The crowd was rabid. She could almost smell their bloodlust.

She reconstructed the road she trod upon from memory, paved and wide enough here for four horses. Ignoring the jeering mob, her mind filled in what she could not see. The province of Rhagae was not incredibly large, but it was well situated on the trade route and very rich. With sturdy gates and the snowy

Elburz Mountains to the north, it seemed impossible to breach. But she and her army had found a way.

"This is the Queen of Warriors?" a woman asked in Aramaic. "I thought she'd be taller and her hair golden."

"Where are her horns?" a girl asked.

"I heard she's an Amazon," another said. "They say she fights as well as a man."

"Well, she has muscles enough like a man," the first said. "And look at that gash on her arm!"

"I hope King Artaxerxes pours salt on it before he impales her," the girl said.

The Queen of Warriors . . . She had not thought of herself that way since losing her cavalry and all her men at Aegis three years before. But now she slipped the persona on as she would a well-worn pair of sandals she had long ago discarded. *I will die as the Queen of Warriors, as I was meant to.*

She sensed the danger a moment before it came. A stone flew through the air and pelted her leather breastplate. Another hit her boot, and a third struck her forearm—that one stung. The guards moved to protect her, their scent of sweat, myrrh, and leather enveloping her as they raised their shields. A few stones pinged against metal, but then a deep voice announced that anyone who hurt the Queen of Warriors would lose a hand. The crowd quieted. The danger had passed. She raised her head high, remembering who she had once been.

"It will take more than a few pebbles to kill the Queen of Warriors!" she shouted in her battle voice, then laughed as the guards scrambled to protect her.

Soon the heat of the sun was replaced by the cool of the fortress. The rope went slack for a moment, then was taken up by another. Artaxerxes must have dismounted. Was he leading her into his fortress to exhibit her to his men?

"Stairs," a guard growled, grabbing her elbow and leading her up.

She pictured the oxblood columns holding up the great archway which led into a vast courtyard and attempted to recall the layout—the audience chamber, the dining halls, and the stone stairs leading to the maze of rooms on the upper floors. She had not thought of this fortress in years, but she tried to envision where she was now—and to guess in what room her torture would take place.

Sensing a moment of laxity on the part of the guards, she elbowed the one nearest her and almost pulled off the blindfold before another caught her from behind.

"Watch her carefully," a Judean said. The sound of a Judean in charge surprised her, and she was unprepared when a potion was brought to her lips.

"Drink," the Judean commanded. She clamped her mouth shut and struggled until a blow to her stomach made her gasp in pain, and a bitter liquid was forced down her throat. She choked and sputtered, then fell into a deep sleep.

* * *

The Queen of Warriors is available now.

ABOUT THE AUTHOR

Zenobia Neil was named after an ancient warrior queen who fought against the Romans. A lifelong lover of Greco-Roman mythology, she writes about the ancient world and gods having too much fun. An English teacher by day, Zenobia spends her time imagining interesting people and putting them in terrible situations. She lives with her husband, two children, and dog in Los Angeles. *Psyche Unbound* is her first book. Visit her at ZenobiaNeil.com